One Man and His Bomb

Also by HRF Keating

Inspector Ghote Series

The Perfect Murder
Inspector Ghote's Good Crusade
Inspector Ghote Caught in Meshes
Inspector Ghote Hunts the Peacock
Inspector Ghote Plays a Joker
Inspector Ghote Breaks an Egg
Inspector Ghote Goes by Train
Inspector Ghote Trusts the Heart
Bats Fly Up for Inspector Ghote
Filmi, Filmi Inspector Ghote
Inspector Ghote Draws a Line
The Murder of the Maharajah
Go West Inspector Ghote
The Sheriff of Bombay
Under a Monsoon Cloud
The Body in the Billiard Room
Dead on Time
The Iciest Sin
Inspector Ghote, His Life and Crimes
Cheating Death
Doing Wrong
Asking Questions
Bribery, Corruption Also
Breaking and Entering

One Man and His Bomb

H. R. F. KEATING

St. Martin's Minotaur

NEW YORK

THOMAS DUNNE BOOKS.
An imprint of St. Martin's Press

www.thomasdunnebooks.com
www.minotaurbooks.com

Library of Congress Cataloging-in-Publication Data
Keating, H. R. F. (Henry Reymond Fitzwalter), 1926–
    One man and his bomb / H.R.F. Keting. –1st St. Martin's Minotaur ed.
        p. cm.
    ISBN-13: 978-0-312-34988-2
    ISBN-10: 0-312-34988-2
    1. Martens, Harriet (Fictitious character)—Fiction. 2. Policewomen—England—London—Fiction. 3. Terrorism—Fiction. 4. Bioterrorism—Fiction. 5. Mothers and sons—Fiction. 6. Twins—Fiction. I. Title.

PR6061.E26O54 2006
823'.914—dc22

                                                                2005056096

First published in Great Britain by Allison & Busby Limited

First St. Martin's Minotaur Edition: August 2006

10 9 8 7 6 5 4 3 2 1

HRF KEATING is well versed in the worlds of crime, fiction and non-fiction. He was the crime books reviewer for *The Times* for fifteen years, as well as serving as the chairman of the Crime Writers' Association and the Society of Authors, and for many years as president of the Detection Club. Best known for his Inspector Ghote series, which twice won him the CWA Gold Dagger Award, in 1996 he was awarded the CWA Cartier Diamond Dagger for outstanding service to crime fiction. He lives in London with his wife, the actress Sheila Mitchell.

One Man and His Bomb

Unmistakably, there came a rumble of distant thunder. Detective Superintendent Harriet Martens, whisky-and-ginger in hand, exhausted after a long day, straightened up with a jerk. Opposite, John, back from his labours at mighty Majestic Insurance, six o'clock glass of chardonnay beside him, gave her a raised-eyebrows look.

'Oh, nothing,' she said. 'Perhaps I'm nervy after these past few days. Or, maybe I'm just not expecting thunder, out of a clear sky. It'd be less surprising if it were next month, before an April shower. But – I don't know – it seemed somehow…foreboding.'

'The Hard Detective feeling threatened by a faraway peal of thunder?'

'I thought,' Harriet replied with a touch of snappishness, 'we had a pact you'd never mention that label they put on me back when I was in B Division stamping on petty crime.'

'Sorry, sorry. We did have a pact. Old habit, teasing you. And you're right, thunder often does seem threatening. But it only seems so. Perhaps because everything, when you come to look at it, is always slightly threatening.'

'Everything? Always?'

'Oh, yes. Being threatened's a condition of life, I often think. There's always something. Who'd have thought, over there in Hasselburg last week just as EuroVin, joyful celebration of wines, was about to begin, that those huge casks each contained an explosive device? Hundreds of deaths.'

'God, yes. We should have switched on the News. There might have been more facts. How could I have pushed it all away, even for a moment? When my workload's suddenly gone through the roof? And perhaps at last got to be worthwhile.'

'I'm glad to hear you say that. You were getting to be fairly boring, on and on about Birchester's non-existent terror precautions. What was that nice phrase you had about your duties? Yes. Busy, you said, building ivory bomb shelters.'

'Well, it's what I was doing. But Hasselburg's changed all that. If al-Qaeda's going to aim at intimidating us simply by killing as many people as they can, they could quite possibly target Birchester. We're not such a different city from Hasselburg, even though we haven't been – what was it al-Qaeda said? – *making a god of forbidden wine*.'

'You're right, of course. Hasselburg's changed everything, if it wasn't in fact the bombs in Madrid that did that.'

'So here am I, suddenly worked to a frazzle, checking security at the football stadiums, gingering up the Railway Police, locating all of Birchester's share of immigrants, innocent or possibly not.'

She gave an ironic grunt of a laugh.

'And only a week ago I was asking myself what there was here as a possible terrorist target. The university? A handful of big factories making what they call consumer disposables? That Heronsgate place, the Government agriculture research lab over in Boreham? Hardly worth any terrorist's while, that.'

'Could attract anti-vivisectionists.'

'That's different. And in any case that piece in the *Star* the other day about some tremendously effective herbicide they've discovered actually mentioned they never used animal testing.'

'You're right about that. But you seem to have missed the follow-up.'

'Probably came straight after Hasselburg. I haven't seen the wretched paper since then. What have I missed?'

'That the people at Heronsgate House are supposed to have gone on to experiment a bit too vigorously with their herbicide. I don't know how the *Star* found out, or even if the story was accurate, but they said its genes were manipulated to the point where the stuff began to multiply unstoppably. Something like what happened in California when they created by mistake a hyper virulent form of tuberculosis. Now there's a real threat, if you like.'

'Point taken. Threat number forty thousand and eight.'

'OK. So that peal of thunder just now can mean anything you like to make of it. It could even portend something cosily pleasant.'

'I don't think so. These aren't cosy days.'

'I know what you mean. We're menaced, no getting away from it. But, it's still true that all threats aren't necessarily of evil. Some are simply bugaboos, which my dictionary calls *sources of groundless fear or dread*. That's why people watch horror films. To have a nice safe shiver. Or even it's when, years ago, we took the twins to that awful pantomime *Babes in the Wood*. Remember? They loved seeing the wicked Baron send the two babes into the horrid forest because somehow they knew, aged four or five, that the birds would come along and cover them with nice warm leaves.'

Harriet raised her glass in a mock toast.

'May all our threats be bugaboos.'

And the phone rang.

For a long moment she sat and looked at it.

'You going to pick it up?' John asked, grinning. 'It's nearest you.'

'Yes. Yes, of course. But are you expecting a call?'

'Much more likely to be duty for you. Unless it's one of your mates wanting a girly gossip. Life must go on, you know, despite Hasselburg.'

'All right. Only one way to find out.'

Harriet pushed herself to her feet and went over.

But she found her mouth contracting into a tiny grimace as she recited the number.

'Mrs Piddock?' asked a male voice she could not recognise.

'Yes. This is Harriet Piddock.'

There was a short silence at the far end. A gathering of

something. Thoughts collected? Some announcement re-
formulated? Courage being plucked up?

'Mrs Piddock. This is Superintendent Charles Robertson,
in charge at Notting Hill police station.'

Notting Hill. Thoughts went scrambling and scuttling
through Harriet's head.

Notting Hill PS, where Malcolm and Graham were in
their first posting since they decided to enter the police and
serve in the Met. Why is this...this Superintendent
Robertson calling about them? Some misdemeanour? Joint
misdemeanour?

But the superintendent's heavy voice was ploughing on.

'Mrs Piddock, I'm afraid it's bad news. Very bad. It's your
son, Graham. I'm sorry to say he's— He has been the
victim of a booby trap. He— He's been killed, Mrs
Piddock. And— And PC Malcolm Piddock, who was with
him at the time, has been seriously injured.'

Harriet felt her whole world turned in an instant upside
down.

It was as if a huge sheet of rusted iron had been swung,
between one moment and the next, through a whole
hundred and eighty degrees, carrying her with it into a
totally different existence. An existence filled to every last
corner with blank, black, overwhelming grief. There was
nothing anywhere. Nothing. Nothing but utter loss.

But in her right ear, she knew, that leaden voice was
plodding onwards, dealing out the facts. Somehow she had
become two people. There was the one who was truly her,
in that new different world, grief-struck, grief-filled. And
there was another. There was someone, something,
altogether like her, but not her. A hologram. Something
made out of a criss-crossing of innumerable laser beams. A
non-person, yet capable of doing whatever a person does.
Of listening to that ongoing, thumping voice, of taking in
what it was telling her, of making the right brief noises of
acknowledgement. Of all that, but nothing else.

Chapter Two

Hologram Harriet heard John asking, with a note of quick anxiety, whether she was all right.

'You've gone absolutely white. Harriet, what is it? What is it?'

And the hologram was able to answer, putting the phone handset back on its rest as if the call had been no more than one from one of her mates, as John had called them.

She turned to face him.

'John, that was the man in charge at Notting Hill police station, a Superintendent Someone-or-other. John, it's Graham. And Malcolm too, really. Graham's been killed by some sort of a bomb. And Malcolm, who was with him, is in Intensive Care at St Mary's, Paddington. He's unconscious, and... And they fear the worst.'

'But what happened? What bomb? What sort of a bomb?'

'They haven't got the full evidence yet, of course. But apparently the boys were *proceeding along Ladbroke Walk*. That was what he actually said, Superintendent, yes, Robertson. It's a sort of mews just behind the police station, and they were on their way to take the tube to Marble Arch to be on anti-terrorist patrol on the platforms there. It seems they'd been doing that duty for several days, and were in the habit of making their way to Notting Hill tube along that traffic-free back-lane. And from how they were lying when they were found— It— It looks as if they were investigating some sort of parcel or package put outside the door of one of the houses there. It was a booby trap, they think. They're sure. And Graham must have moved it and set off the explosion. Or – Superintendent Robertson was a bit confused about it – the explosion may have been set off from a distance just as they got there.'

John, she saw now – the hologram saw – had gone as white as she herself must be.

'But why them? Why our sons? Both. Both of them.'

Abruptly he got to his feet. 'No. We must go. To Malcolm. Get down to London as fast as we can. He might— He might be— What time is it? Yes, not seven yet. Harriet, you're not still on duty, are you? We could set off now, straight away, and be there by ten at the latest?'

She heard herself give a harsh bark of a laugh. She realised then that John, however impulsively he was behaving, had remembered the answerphone and was putting a message on it before hurrying her out to the garage and the car.

She was scarcely aware of anything more as John drove, at and beyond the limit, through the cold of late evening, stars glinting, down the motorway, heading for London and St Mary's, Paddington, where Malcolm was perhaps on the very point of death. Real Harriet and Hologram Harriet merged into one blankness.

At last she was conscious that they had arrived. That John had found a space to park, whether illegally or legally, right outside St Mary's. Stumblingly, she followed him, confused by the street lights and shadows, as he strode over to an illuminated map of the hospital complex. With a jabbing finger he located the words *Intensive Care*, wheeled her round, went back into the street, marched along to an entrance-arch and pointed, like an over-dramatic actor, to the illuminated Queen Elizabeth the Queen Mother building. Then, striding with her into the darkness past other dimmer unlit buildings – there was a flower shop, Hologram Harriet noticed – he crossed an internal road without looking to either side, swept past a tall bronze statue of a wounded wartime Civil Defence worker nursing a naked foot and pushed open some double glass doors.

A barked question to the security man behind the desk and, almost without being aware of how she had got there, Harriet found herself looking through a wide tinted window at an appallingly still figure, heavily bandaged, that she had been told was Malcolm. Tubes were in each nostril, a drip was feeding into an arm, another fat transparent plastic tube lolled inside the mouth, wires were fastened to flesh here and there. Just beyond, a blue line on a VDU screen was ominously darting and quivering. Something else was emitting occasional little bleeps. A green-clad doctor bending forwards was doing something Harriet could not, mercifully, make out to the horribly inert body.

That was Malcolm. Malcolm. Still, at least, alive.

Malcolm was holding his own, so a sympathetic blue-tunic nurse told them. But he was by no means out of danger. Apart from multiple injuries to the lower half of his body, she said, he had sustained a single more serious one when a small flying piece of metal had penetrated his head. It had been successfully removed, but it had left him in a coma.

Little of the medical jargon meant much to Harriet. All that she took in was that there was hope still. The threat of the unthinkable end – unthinkable, but all too urgently present – was only hovering, still at a distance. A short, short distance.

It must have been a long time later that she felt John take her arm at the elbow and begin to steer her away.

'I've been having a word when the chap looking after him came out for a break,' he said in a whisper. 'I don't think you even noticed. But he says there's little point in our staying on. Either he'll...'

She knew what he was telling her. Knew all too well.

Still steering her, he led the way down steps, round corners, down other stairs, until they arrived at the brightly-lit entrance lobby once more.

And there, left on a ledge, was a discarded newspaper with blazoned across its front page, impossible to miss, *PC Twins in Terror Bomb Blast.*

John snatched it up, for a moment made as if to hide it from her sight, then realised that there was no point. He stood there in the light of the neon tube overhead, his eyes tearing into the short account under that somehow dagger-like headline. At last he looked up.

'Nothing more really than we know already,' he said. 'It's tomorrow's *Banner*. Must be the edition they print for

Scotland, quite early in the evening. There's hardly any detail about what exactly happened. Just the facts. But— But how the hell did they get hold of this about the victims being twins? That damned awful human-interest touch?'

His face momentarily contracted in anger, sheer exhaustion overcoming his customary control.

He pushed the paper back on the shelf, shoved open the glass doors and stepped with Harriet into the cuttingly chill night outside.

'Look,' he said, as they stood there, 'I'm really not fit to drive back home. I don't think I was even fit to drive down here. I suppose I may just manage now to get the car to somewhere safe to park. But then I'm going to find a hotel and hope to get some sleep before going back up tomorrow. Will you stay down here with me?'

Harriet thought, tried to think.

'No,' she said at last. 'John, I want to go home. Home. Couldn't you…?'

'Darling, I can't. I just wouldn't be safe on the road. I absolutely can't. But if you really do want to get back home, that's Paddington Station looming at the end of the road there. I think there should be a late train. Could you manage that? What do you think?'

'Yes,' she answered, 'Yes, I would like to be at home, somehow I feel…'

John went with her then along to the big empty echoing station. They found the last train to Birchester was due to leave in seven minutes. A ticket to be bought. The platform to be located. Then she was leaning out of the carriage window, making a pale effort to wave towards John's dark figure as the train moved away.

She fell back on the seat behind her and sat there.

Before long she realised that tears were rolling down her cheeks. On and on. Impossible to stop, even if she had the will to halt them. Impossible to stop, even if opposite her there had been a row of concerned and curious travellers.

There were no thoughts behind the outpouring. A total

inner blankness. The mere feeling of intolerable pain.

Then perhaps sleep, of a sort. Or mere oblivion.

And a porter opening the carriage door.

'Birchester, madam. Far as this one goes. You all right?'

'Yes, yes. I'm...I just need a cab, if there is one.'

'Oh, yes, should be. I'll see you to it. Nothing else to do, this time of night.'

She woke, as she always did, at seven. For a few minutes, unusually, she simply lay where she was. And she found there were still two Harriets there in her head, not even side by side but superimposed one on the other. The real one, still weighed-down with grief. The hologram, emotionless, able to think rationally about what Harriet should be doing.

Go into Headquarters? Carry on with her attempts to counter the possible threat of a terrorist attack in Birchester? But no. A terrible blow had been delivered to her, to her and to John. She could not be expected to work in any calm, orderly way. No one, in fact when they heard on the radio what had happened or read about it in the *Birchester Chronicle*, would expect to find her in her office.

But she must have news.

Malcolm. Had he got through the rest of the night? Ring St Mary's? No. No, John will almost certainly be there already, or will be very soon. And the moment he knows anything he'll ring me. So, wait.

And, yes, Hologram Harriet said to herself, I must get up now, shower, be ready to cope with whatever has to be done, eat a good breakfast. Or however much I can.

Stepping out of the shower, feeling a little better though unable not to rebuke herself for perhaps having cast away a particle of mourning, she heard the phone shrilling. At once Hologram Harriet realised the answerphone must still be on.

God, I forgot last night that John switched it on. What if I miss...?

Towel clutched round her, she ran wet-footed downstairs, rushed to the machine, still ringing, seized the receiver.

'Yes? Yes?'

'Harriet?' came John's measured voice. 'Good morning, and good news. Or as good as can be expected. Malcolm's still unconscious. But his condition's stable, they say. They can't, or won't, make any predictions about the future. But, they tell me, every hour that he stays in his present state the better's the long-term outlook.'

These were words that penetrated now past the hologram figure. She felt a dam-burst of healing water wash over and over her.

'Oh, John, thank God. Oh, that's wonderful.'

Her hologram self took in that the glowing red figures of the answerphone were registering zero. So no night calls. Mechanically she put a finger on the power button. The machine's cool female voice intoned 'Answer off.'

'Well, don't let yourself be too optimistic,' she heard John saying. 'They warned me there could still be brain damage. Too early to tell. You know, when someone's as badly injured as Malcolm, something can always happen that the doctors can't foresee. His life could still be threatened.'

'Yes, yes. You're right. They're right. But— But I'm going to hope. I can't help myself.'

'No, and neither can I. Hope's the opposite of threat, you know. Hope and threat, they're both in there fighting it out.'

'Oh, yes. Yes, you're right. And thank you for saying it.'

'OK. Well, I'm going to set off in just a few minutes, when I've tackled the Full British Breakfast they say I'm owed. It's a nice day here, so I should make good time. But I think I ought to go straight to the office, let them know I'm available if needed. The insurance industry has to go grinding on, you know, counteracting some of the disasters that do occur. But you? You're not going in to your Headquarters, are you?'

'Well, no. No, I was just thinking I wouldn't, though I'd

better get in touch to say so.'

'Right, well, see you shortly then. And— And, darling, try to find your way back to life, if you can.'

'Yes. Yes, I will. Or, no, I'll try. But— But, John, Graham.' She checked a sob. 'Graham gone. Gone for ever.'

The receiver went down with a clunk.

And at once the phone beneath her hand rang out piercingly.

It took her some seconds to pick it up again and shut off the insistent ringing.

'Mrs Piddock?' a top-of-the-morning voice sang out. 'Mrs Harriet Piddock? Birchester Television here.'

'Yes?' she said, hardly knowing she had done so.

'Mrs Piddock, we were wondering if you would like to come into the studio this morning and record an interview.'

Harriet felt bewilderment go chasing, zig-zag, through her mind.

'I— I'm sorry?' she said.

A deep, suffering breath at the far end. *Can't the foolish woman understand the simplest thing?*

'Mrs Piddock, surely you want to tell people about this tragedy? How the outrage has affected you? I mean, you'll want to make everybody realise, the Government and everybody, that terrorism has got to be stopped. So, can we send a car for you at, say, twelve o'clock?'

'No.'

Once again she put down the handset. But this time with all the unhurried decisiveness of an official stamping out an order to quit.

But if she had thought that her spat-out *No* had been enough to put an end to Birchester Television's plans, she was soon to learn they had more shots in their locker.

Half an hour later, when she had just pushed away her bowl of cereal, half-eaten, the phone rang again. She did not, as she went to answer it, envisage for a moment that it would be the brightly cheerful young man who had called her earlier. Hologram Harriet had effectively dealt with him, as Real Harriet had dealt with many a reporter's try-on in the past.

So, as ever, she simply answered the call, and experienced a small shock of surprise at what the secretarial voice at the other end said.

'Mrs Martens? The Assistant Chief Constable would like a word.'

Mr Brown, she thought. Perhaps I should have let him know earlier than this that I must have some leave. I would probably have done so already, except for that Birchester Television man.

She heard the ACC coming on the line.

'Mrs Piddock,' his Scots-tinged voice pronounced, 'let me say at once that you have the sympathy of every man and woman in the CID at your Graham's death. An appalling thing. Appalling. And Malcolm? Do you have any up-to-date news about him?'

'Yes. Yes, sir. My husband's down there in London and saw the doctors early this morning. He told me Malcolm's got through the night all right, and they're a little more hopeful.'

'I gather he was very severely injured, though. Is that right?'

'Yes, sir. I saw him myself last night, and— And, yes, he did seem to be in...In a very bad state.'

'Well, let's hope. Hope and pray.'

She remembered then that the ACC was a practising Christian, brought up indeed in the severest Scottish traditions.

'Thank you, sir,' she managed to reply.

'Now, of course, Mrs Martens, you are relieved of your duties at the present. Yes, at the present. But...'

He paused so long that she felt obliged to put in a 'Yes, sir?'

A cough.

'Mrs Martens, a few minutes ago I had a call from Birchester Television. They told me they had wanted to interview you, but that you had refused. Categorically.'

A quiet rolling of Scots r's.

'Now, I am going to ask you to change that decision. No, don't tell me to mind my own business, though I am sure the words are on your lips. But let me first say that I see it as your duty as a police officer, whatever unpleasantness may be involved, to expose yourself to this.'

'Sir—'

'No. I haven't finished. You and your sons have become, however unfairly, victims of the enemy in what they call the War on Terror. It is a war – in so far as that's the right word for it – which the Police Service is required to fight in whatever ways are necessary. And I am suggesting to you now that your appearance on television is one of those necessities. We are not alone in this fight. Every decent citizen in this country, and in others, is involved. Many of them, however, do not as yet recognise that. But you, appearing on their screens this evening, and telling them what you and your sons have suffered at the hands of these deluded individuals, can make a considerable difference. No, *will* make a considerable difference.'

Harriet stood in silence, the phone held hard to her ear.

'Very well, sir,' she said at last. 'If you put it to me in those terms, of course there is nothing else I can do but accept.'

'Very good, Harriet. I'll get back to these people and arrange for them to get in touch with you.'

So shortly before six that evening Harriet was led into the make-up room at the TV station for an interview to appear almost immediately on the local News. She submitted then, not by any means for the first time, to being told that her nose was shiny and needed powdering, and to having her hair, which despite everything she had managed neatly to deal with earlier, being combed and teased into a shape that pleased the make-up girl.

It was only when, in purely thoughtless innocence, the girl asked if she would like her cheeks given a touch of colour because she was looking 'a bit pale' that she rebelled. And even then she managed to contain herself.

'No. No, thank you. I think I'm better as I am.'

Then she was taken to the studio and patiently went through all the changes of position and angle the cameraman asked for.

The interview itself began smoothly enough. The glib words of condolence were spoken and Hologram Harriet acknowledged them with a stiff dip of her head.

Soon she was asked – in crude terms, she could not help thinking – what exactly had happened to Malcolm. And she managed to take shelter behind a lack of knowledge of the actual facts and avoid giving the grim particulars of what, the night before in the intensive care ward, had so appalled her.

'And your other son,' the interviewer asked, plunging on, 'he was killed instantly, wasn't he?'

If you know, she thought with steely fury, why do you have to ask me?

'Yes,' she shot out.

Across the gloom that divided her from the interviewer, each of them in their separate pools of light, she thought she could see in his face much the same *Christ, can't you react a bit for me?* expression that he had sent down the phone to her first thing in the morning.

But she saw no reason why she should provide him with spilled-out words that would allow him afterwards to pat himself on the back and say he thought his interview had gone 'pretty well'.

Other questions followed. None of them, as far as she could see, rightly phrased to give her a proper chance to bring out the depths of the misery she was feeling, depths which the ACC had wanted her to make the watching public feel. Feel and react to.

She caught, as she produced a few more laboured words, her interviewer giving a swift glance at the big studio clock.

It must all be coming to an end. And, all right, Mr Brown

hadn't got the responses he wanted to fire viewers with determination to combat the reckless forces poised to bring devastation.

Well, too bad. I'm a police officer, not a bloody actor milking outrage.

'Mrs Piddock, as a mother with one son dead and the other terribly wounded, what is it you feel at this moment about the people who made that bomb?'

This my chance after all?

But the blunt insensitivity of the question produced in her, in Real Harriet, something absolutely unexpected. Totally from nowhere.

'Yes,' her answer shot out. 'Yes, one of my sons is dead. And the other is so badly injured they fear for his life, if not his sanity. And you, you sit there, expecting me to denounce the people who did that, expecting me to say we must all *go to war* against any axis of evil we can find in the world. To fight it and obliterate it. But I am not going to do that. I've scarcely been able to think in the single day that's gone by since my sons suffered so awfully. But one thing I do know. However evil, evil as people say, men such as these are, and women too, women, they do not do what they are doing, here and all over the world, out of some mere wish to kill and to maim. They do it, rightly or wrongly, because they feel they have a grievance. A deep grievance. And it is up to us, those of us who so far have escaped injury at their hands, and those of us who have not, to look at those grievances. To ask ourselves whether our unthinking attitudes and actions over the years have created the menaces that hover now above all of us. Then, when we have seen what it is that motivates what we so easily label evil, seen it and have moved to remedy it, then, if you like, we can go marching into war against them. Then, when those grievances have been tackled, and hopefully will be removed, in so far as is possible, then we can feel justified in fighting the enemy that is left.'

Harriet had not felt it possible simply to go home after she had walked out of Birchester Television studios. She had been disoriented, more than a little, by the stream of words that had come from her in answer to that *This is what you should say* question. Instead, she had gone into the first coffee shop that had caught her eye and had sat there in a vacant armchair, statutory cup in front of her, not thinking. Only when at last it had come to her that time had passed did she get up, pay and make her way home.

There she found John, back from his office. He had jumped to his feet at the sound of her key in the door and come rushing out.

'Darling,' he greeted her, 'you were splendid.'

She blinked, for a moment bewildered. Then she realised that he must have been in the house for some time and had switched on the *Six O'Clock News*.

'Splendid? On TV?' she said. 'Was I? I— I scarcely realised what I was saying. But, tell me, was what I did say really *splendid*?'

'It absolutely was. I thought of having a bottle of fizz here to greet you. Until, of course, it came to me that this was no time for any sort of celebration. But I still want to do something. Will a kiss do?'

It did. A long, warm, husbandly embrace.

'Yes,' John said, releasing her, 'it couldn't have been better put. Certainly to my way of thinking. In fact, it anticipated what I'd not got round to working out.'

'No, I hadn't worked anything out either. I could scarcely think all day of anything but that one bleak, blank fact. Graham's dead. Graham's dead.'

Graham's dead. In a deluge the whole meaning of it poured back into her mind. The blank blackness blotting out everything.

But she saw, she was able to see, that John was looking at

her, concern plain on his every feature. And it was that which dragged her back from the heavy depths.

She shook her head clear.

'It— It was only when—' she said. 'It was only when that interviewer – I suppose I'm meant to know his name – only when he put that crudely expressed question to me that it penetrated, all in one instant, right down to the thought that had been growing there in the depths of my mind. And you think I was right? You think what I thought then, what I said in reply to him, was right?'

'I do. I did. If last weekend, only last weekend, I'd been asked after the Hasselburg horror, what I believed was the answer to it all, I'd have probably groped towards just what you came bursting out with. Darling, I could positively see it coming rushing up to the surface from – what? – your brain? No, from your heart.'

She felt a pale smile appearing on her lips, in her eyes.

'Only you wouldn't have been quite so incoherent,' she managed mildly to joke.

A smile in return.

'No. No, I admit what you said may not have been expressed with the utmost clarity. But what you meant came over without the least tinge of confusion. I know it did. And all the people watching – well, most of them – will know what it was you came out with. Well done, well done, well done.'

But then, once more, the jangling phone wanted its say.

Malcolm, she thought. Oh God, don't let it be St Mary's and bad news, the worst news.

John, after one quick glance at her suddenly apprehensive face, picked up the receiver.

'Yes. Yes, she's here. But—' He listened for a moment. 'Oh, yes, I can certainly give her a message.'

He paid attention again.

'Yes. All right, I'll tell her.'

He put down the receiver.

'That was your Assistant Commissioner's secretary. He

wants to see you in his office at eleven tomorrow morning.'

She dropped into a chair, legs suddenly unable to support her.

'What— What do you...? I mean, he's going to be furious. He wanted me to do the interview so as to alert people to the dangers that have come to hover over them. I— I sort of said that's what I would do. It was only when...'

'Darling, I know. And until you get to see him... What did that girl say his name was? I've forgotten.'

'No wonder. It's Brown, plain Andrew Brown. But he's by no means the ordinary man-in-the-street that might imply. I've always found him distinctly impressive, the comparatively little I've had directly to do with him.'

'Well, we'll see what Mr Brown's reaction will be when you hear it. His secretary can hardly be expected to indicate what his feelings are.'

'Yes, you're right. But it's a long time to have to wait.'

'With the threat of the great man's displeasure, or even of his active anger, hanging over you? So I'll tell you what we'll do. First of all, I'll pass on what I had meant to tell you all along. I rang St Mary's shortly before you came in, and they said Malcolm's still unconscious but that he is showing some signs of progress. Good news, as far as it goes.'

Harriet felt a pulse of new life go through her. But she was unable to put her feelings into any words.

John went on.

'Now, I'm going to call that take-away place and order us some supper. Then I'm going to go to the medicine cupboard and find you a couple of those sleeping pills I think we've still got. And, finally, you will go to bed, however early it is, and you'll have a long, long restorative sleep.'

Still blurrily affected next morning by a night of dreadful dreams, Harriet seemed only to half-hear the Scots' voice coming from the far side of the wide desk.

'Very well, Superintendent,' it pronounced, 'I can't say

that last night you provided exactly what I had hoped to hear. But I can well understand how it burst out. If those people in television stopped for even a moment to think what they were doing... However, they don't, and we must live with the results. So, let me say, I agreed with every word I heard. And, let me add, that I forbid you to tell any soul beyond these four walls that I said so. A senior police officer cannot go mouthing off with his any and every opinion. That sort of conduct can be left to officers stepping out of a courtroom after they've secured a conviction and telling the world how *evil* the man or woman is who's just been put away. And they wouldn't do that if I had my way.'

Harriet gave the man opposite, solidly seated there in his pale grey suit, plain blue tie, white shirt with its thin blue stripe, a quiet smile of relief, and of gratitude.

'But,' he went on unbendingly, 'we'll say no more about that. I've something else to put to you. Something altogether different.'

Better adjusted now to his hanging-in-air pauses, Harriet allowed half a second to go by, and then produced her 'Yes, sir?'

But she still was not to get a reply.

'Aye,' it came eventually, and heavily.

Another pause. But a much shorter one.

'Now, Harriet, you know well what pressure the whole of Greater Birchester Police is under. Every man and woman on the alert, as a prime duty, for any sign that we're going to be made into another Hasselburg. You'll know about that as much as anyone, with all you've been doing these past weeks. And don't think your efforts have gone without recognition. Still, that's by-the-by. What I have to tell you... What I have to ask you, despite the trouble you're in, is whether you're fit to be tasked, here and now, with something else, something altogether more like active police work?'

Christ, Harriet thought, what has this man of granite got

in his head now? Jesus, I've just had a son of mine horribly killed. I've another lying in hospital with the threat of death hanging over him. Or, perhaps worse, the threat of becoming a mindless zombie. And there he is, sitting on the other side of this big desk of his, proposing that I should undertake an active investigation.

'Aye, I see you're thinking I'm an unfeeling block of wood. And I misdoubt whether I am or not. But think of this. However terrible the trouble you're in, the trouble any one of us is in, there is something that can help us out of it. Help you out of it. And that's work. Work. It's what we poor wee creatures are put on God's earth to do, and when trouble comes the more we do it and the sooner we do it, the more it helps us out of those troubles.'

There was a part of Harriet, the hologram part, that knew what Andrew Brown had said had in it more than a little truth.

'I expect you're right, sir,' she answered him. 'Only... Well, yes, I do expect you're right.'

'Very good. Now, let me tell you something in the strictest confidence.'

'Sir?'

'You must know Heronsgate House, the agricultural research station.'

Heronsgate House. And wasn't I saying to John, just before all this happened, that the place was anything but a target for terrorists. What is this?

'Yes, I know it, sir.'

'Perhaps you know, too, that they recently produced there an extremely effective herbicide. So, what – bevy of mad scientists that they are – did they do? They set out further to manipulate it, and contrived to produce an unstoppable runaway substance, several thousand times more effective than the original.'

'My husband told me there was a story about that in the *Star*,' Harriet put in. 'He said what they'd done paralleled something that happened in California, I think it was, where they altered a tuberculosis bacterium and caused that, too, to run amok.'

'I dare say they did. However, the story in the *Star* happens to be the simple truth. And, of course, the lab at Heronsgate House was ordered to destroy the stuff once and for all. But, as you won't find it hard to believe, they've delayed in carrying out that instruction. Fond of their pet discovery, I suppose.'

Into Harriet's mind there flashed a horrible suspicion.

'They want to conduct some sort of trial of it, sir?'

'If that were all... No, last night, or half an hour before midnight on Tuesday to be exact, a gang of criminals broke into the place and stole from the Director's own office the one specimen of the stuff in existence.'

The implications spread through Harriet's mind as rapidly as the stolen specimen itself might do were it released.

'Sir,' she said, 'if the work you had in mind for me is investigating the break-in there, then I'm ready to start at once.'

'Aye. I thought I'd not be wrong to ask you. But, first, listen to this. If any sort of word gets out of the threat that's hanging over the whole of Birchester, then we're more than likely to be in for as nasty a panic as anything al-Qaeda has brought about. Worse, even. Up to now we've succeeded in informing people anent terrorist threats to be provident rather than induce panic. But when something comes as near to home as Heronsgate House, that will alter. It's because of that danger I am tasking you, you alone, with all the initial investigation.'

Again the implications spread through Harriet's mind.

'Sir, you can rely on me,' she said at last.

'I hope so. They used to call you the Hard Detective, as I recollect. Well, I'm giving you a hard task, working on your own. As hard a task as any you had back when you earned that name. But I believe you'll be up to it. Yes, up to it, at least till we've found out the full extent of the danger.'

He looked down for a moment at the uncluttered surface of his wide desk.

'Very well then, you'll be wanting to get over there to that Heronsgate place as soon as you can. So I won't keep you. Oh, but yes, I will, for a moment. When the Chief was told about this – the Director at Heronsgate House had got in touch with an official at the Home Office – he was given a name as a possible perpetrator. A certain Ernst Wichmann, former Professor of German Studies at the University here. No more than that. But you had better take a look at him.'

'Yes, sir.'

'And remember this. If your personal circumstances now become too onerous, if indeed you need urgently to visit your injured son, let me know at once. I'll not stand in your way.'

Harriet forced herself to hold back the tears she instantly had thought would come.

'Thank you, sir.'

And left.

John at Majestic, she said to herself, would have to be given a carefully worded message.

Heronsgate House, Harriet remembered as she brought her car to a halt outside, had once been a private school for girls. On the edge of Birchester, swept past by a later flood of boxy building, it had since been put to a series of different purposes. The last of which, made plain by a tall shiny chimney rising up over it, was this research institute. Sitting gathering herself together, she realised that Mr Brown had done more for her than simply task her with a serious confidential inquiry. He had, in the course of the hammering quarter of an hour she had been with him, forced her hologram image and her real self back together once more into one fully active organism.

Yes, she thought, I now have Graham's killing, Malcolm's mutilation, lodged somewhere in my head where I can look steadily at them both. Andrew Brown's treatment of me was something I could never have submitted to of my own will. But, done now, it's left me – I know it – stronger than I could possibly have believed.

She got out of the car, locked it and marched up the short, dustily gravelled drive of the house, the keen March wind tugging at the skirts of her coat.

Before she reached the wide front door with its arched overhead window and its flight of unwashed, whitish steps in a wide arc, from round the side of the house two men appeared. At once she recognised from the long, bright-blue, brass-buttoned overcoats they were wearing that they must belong to a local security firm, dignified by the name Birchester Watchmen.

She came to a halt and watched as they headed for the gate, two burly individuals, one black, the other, from the particular cast of his ruddy face, perhaps Irish.

She let them get to within a few yards of her, and then, seizing the opportunity, spoke.

'Good morning, am I right in thinking you're on duty here?'

They stopped, the black man less quickly than his companion. But it was the latter who answered.

'What's that to you?'

Yes, thickish Irish accent.

'Greater Birchester Police, Detective Superintendent Martens.'

Quick looks from one to the other.

Well, security guards are often even more involved with the lower criminal ranks than detective constables are.

'Nothing to worry about,' she said. 'But I understand there was a break-in here last night. I'm making inquiries.'

'You're right about the break-in,' the Irishman replied. 'We were on duty here last night, me mate an' meself, an' we bore the brunt of it.'

Harriet did her best to disguise her quickening interest.

'So, tell me what happened,' she said. 'Are you here reporting about it?'

'We are so,' the Irishman answered. 'And I'll tell you what happened. I'll show you. Here, Winston, let the lady see your face.'

Winston visibly hesitated.

'Go on, matey, let the lady have a good look.'

Reluctantly he approached and, turning down the thick collar of his coat – yes, a *Birchester Watchmen* shoulder-flash – tilted his head so that a dark area of broken bruising was visible.

'Oh yes,' Harriet said, anxious to reassure the fellow enough to get him to talk freely, 'that looks nasty.'

'Sure it does,' the Irish guard put in. 'Nasty as can be. An' that's not all. Not by a long way.'

'Have you got bruises to show, too?'

'Bruises? I was damn near being a burnt corpse, so I was.'

'Burnt? How was that?'

'They only doused me head to foot with petrol. Tied me there, an' told old Winston they'd put a match to me 'less he gave them his keys.'

She turned to Winston, who looked sheepishly at the gravelly ground by his feet.

'So what did you do?'

'What could he do?' The Irishman broke in. 'Only do the decent thing for his old mate and hand over the whole set. Didn't you, matey? An' what did ye get for your help to the damn lot of them, me old Winny? That club in your face. He was at the hospital half the night, so he was. An' here he is back after reporting, good as gold, to Mr Lennox in his office.'

Winston gave his fellow guard a quick anxious look.

'Yeah,' he said. 'Yeah, I was. At St Ozzies.'

So perhaps he had something to look sheepish about, Harriet thought, having yielded to that threat, however reasonably.

'Yes,' she said to him. 'If that was the situation, with your fellow guard being menaced like that, you did absolutely the right thing. It's always—'

'If that was the situation?' the Irishman banged out. 'Look, lady. Smell this. Smell the coat I have on. The petrol's not gone from it yet. '

He stepped up close and thrust his arm almost into Harriet's face. And, yes, she could smell petrol.

'All right,' she said, 'you had a tough time, both of you.'

For a moment she thought of the tough time she had had herself when, idly chatting with John about the thoughts a peal of thunder could put into your head, the phone had suddenly rung with its obliterating message. Yes, anything like that could leave you for long afterwards as jumpy as this fellow seemed to be.

'We did. So, we did. Didn't we, Winny?'

'Yeah, Mike, yeah.'

'Now, tell me everything you can remember.'

'We have, so we have, every last thing.'

'I don't think so,' she said with a touch of sharpness. 'For example, how many of them were there?'

'Sure, how'd you expect us to tell? Wasn't it all over in a couple of minutes? A ring at the bell. Winston opened up. Didn't think nothing of it. Then wasn't he shoved right out of the way, gun in his belly? An' they were in. Rope over me head an' round me arms before I knew it. An' next the petrol, an' what they said to Winston. How much time d'you think we had to call a fecking roll? An' all in the half-dark. May've been four o' them, may've been only three. Might have been half a dozen behind. Damned if I know. Damned if Winston does.'

'Yeah, I didn't go counting, no more than what Mike did.'

'All right, but you must have had a better look at them when they left. Were they black or white, Asian or what?'

'Do you think I cared a damn what they were?' Mike came back. 'Wasn't it half-dark in the hall there, an' them wid scarves across their faces, rubber gloves on their hands, an' me scared out of me wits all along? How could I tell anything about them? How could Winston?'

'Yeah, yeah,' the black guard quickly agreed.

How dozy can you get, Harriet said to herself. Still, Birchester Watchmen were a cheap outfit, so they might be expected to recruit pretty duff staff.

She sighed.

'All right. But tell me what happened in the end. Did someone find you tied up like that?'

'Not at all, not at all. D'you think I can't get rid of a few ropes that a lot of— That fellas like that put round me wrists?'

'So you managed to release yourself, and Winston after you?'

'That was the way of it, wasn't it, Winny, me lad?'

'Yeah. Yeah.'

'So what time was that? How long were you tied up there?'

Once again Mike produced his hurt and irate look.

'D'you think we were after looking at our watches when we got rid of them ropes? Half-dead as we were?'

Harriet thought for a moment.

Half-dead was right. The two of them must have been half-dead from the time they came on duty. Look at the way Winston went blundering down the instant he heard the door-bell and opened up as if he was welcoming a pizza delivery.

'So, what did you do when you'd got rid of those ropes?' she asked. 'At whatever time it was?'

Mike drew himself up.

'What did I do? I did my duty, that's what. I took poor old Winston straight over to St Ozzies. That's what I did, with him bleeding like a pig.'

'Was he that bad? There isn't any blood on his coat that I can see.'

'I— I—' Winston stammered.

'Sure, didn't they wash it off of him at St Ozzies? What d'you expect of a grand hospital like that?'

And you left this place wide open, Harriet said to herself. Well, I suppose I could expect no better from a couple of dolts like you.

'All right,' she said. 'I'll leave it at that. For the time being. Now, give me your names. I suppose I can always find you again through your office.'

Mike looked more cheerful.

'Sure, you can. Any time at all. Just ask for Michael O'Dowd or Winston Earl, an' they'll bring us up to you, sweet as you like.'

She decided it was a good deal more important to see the Institute Director. If only to discover the circumstances in which he had retained the runaway herbicide and, worse, had kept it where it had been easy enough to steal.

She went up to the big, green-painted, shabby-looking front door and put a firm finger on the button of the round brass bell beside it.

Unpolished, she noted.

Inside, at the mention of her name and rank, the receptionist promptly took her up to the top floor of the house. Past the open door of a small bedroom – tousled duvet and head-dented pillows on the wide bed – past a door marked *Private*, the Director's lavatory presumably. And, next to it, came a door with an impressive metal plaque *Dr Giles Lennox, Director.*

A discreet tap on the panel below that.

'Enter.'

Harriet saw, behind a desk wider even than Andrew Brown's, a neat-featured, pale, smallish man, dark hair clipped short, dressed, slightly surprisingly, in a brown, green-flecked countryman's suit, with a woven green tie at the neck of his checked shirt. The scientist as farmer. Or no, as gentleman farmer.

She had scarcely time, however, to register the discrepancy between the Director's free-and-easy appearance and the single formal *Enter* he had snapped out before, the moment his door been softly closed behind her, in no countryman's burr he began issuing instructions.

'Detective Superintendent Martens, your Assistant Chief

Constable for Crime telephoned me that he was sending you here. Now, let me make it clear, once and for all: the business you have been sent to look into is to be kept absolutely secret. I understand you are reporting solely to Mr Brown, and I emphasise that, *solely*. Not a word is to be said about what has happened to a single other person. In any circumstances. Is that clear?'

Harriet wondered for an instant just how to reply. But she had little difficulty in framing her answer.

'I understand what you are saying. And, subject to Mr Brown's further orders, I will do as you have asked. But, should he give me an order that requires me to tell any other individual what has happened, then I have to say I will do as I am instructed.'

All right, she thought, we've begun on the wrong foot. But so be it. I'm not going to let myself, or Mr Brown, be put under any restrictions by the man who is wholly responsible for the deeply threatening situation caused by his failure to destroy that extraordinarily dangerous substance.

Her eyes flicked immediately to a tall filing cabinet in a smart shade of very pale grey just behind the Director's massive desk. Its deep top drawer, she saw, still half-open, had been wrenched and distorted where some instrument had been used to force it.

Without waiting for any response to what she had said to Dr Lennox, she gestured towards the cabinet.

'That, of course,' she said, 'is where you were keeping the substance your laboratory produced.'

The Director's mouth clamped shut.

'It was in there.'

Is he going to try the say-nothing tactic, she thought. And how to...? Ah, yes. Try this.

'Dr Lennox, I find, quite absurdly, that I do not even know what that substance is called. Mr Brown didn't happen to mention its name when he tasked me this morning. So what do you call it?'

The comparative harmlessness of her question did the trick. Dr Lennox produced a slight smile, not without a touch of superiority.

'It has no name,' he said. 'We simply use CA 534, the number allocated to the experimental procedure which achieved final success.'

Success, Harriet thought. What sort of success was it to have produced, by some error, such destructive runaway stuff?

However, I've got him talking. So keep on with the soft approach.

'On my way in,' she went on, 'I chanced to see the guards from the Birchester Watchmen firm who were on duty here last night. I gathered from them – I understand you have spoken to them as well – that the break-in last night was a distinctly professional job. Can you suggest any criminal, or even terrorist, organisation that might have got to know about this CA 534 and what use it might be put to?'

But Dr Lennox at once fought back.

'Don't you think, Superintendent,' he said sharply, 'that if I had, I would not have informed the Home Office of my suspicions? And they would, of course, have passed on the information to...your superiors?'

So, battle-lines again.

'I have been fully briefed, sir,' she said. 'In fact, I was given the name of a man on file as possibly suspect. That of a former professor at Birchester University, one Ernst Wichmann. Does that name mean anything to you?'

'Wichmann? A German? What else do you know about him?'

Aggressive bugger.

'I asked if you knew him, or of him.'

At that, for an instant, Dr Lennox looked disconcerted. Then in level tones he replied.

'No, Superintendent, I do not think I have ever heard of the gentleman.'

'Very well.'

She paused.

'Now, in the ordinary way,' she said, 'I would be asking you to vacate this office, and—'

'What do you mean *vacate*? It's out of the question that I should not be able to conduct the work of the Institute from this room. Out of the question.'

'I was about to say, sir, that in the particular circumstances of the case, the need to have hundred per cent security concerning the theft, coupled with the fact, as I have ascertained, that the people who broke in here appeared to be professionals, gloved and masked, I think it better to omit the customary forensic checks. People like that are not likely to leave any useful indications.'

She came to a halt. But could not resist adding one small jibe.

'So you can continue with your work, on your CA 534 and whatever else you were expecting to do, undisturbed.'

Slowly the Institute's Director simmered down.

'That will be very helpful,' he said.

'So perhaps you could help me with some facts about how the CA 534 was stored here? Was there no other secure place to put it, if it had to be kept?'

Dr Lennox stiffened a little.

'I gave the matter considerable thought,' he said. 'Naturally. But I came to the conclusion that the fewer people who knew about it and its whereabouts the better. Staff do talk, you know, however firm their instructions to the contrary. Perhaps you read in the *Evening Star* recently what purported to be an account of the discovery we made of CA 491, the predecessor to 534. That was not from any official statement issued to the media.'

'Yes, I read that story.'

She decided not to go on to say she had read, or been told of, the other, more speculative, and more damning, story in the *Star*. And it was plain the Director was by no means prepared to draw her attention to it.

'Very   well,'   he   continued   smoothly.   'In   the circumstances, I thought that the fewest possible number of people who knew where the CA 534 was, or who knew indeed of its existence, the better. Of course, the people who worked on it knew it had been produced, but even they did not know for certain that I had decided it was premature to have it destroyed.'

'This is more than I was told in my briefing this morning,' Harriet said. 'It narrows down the field to a considerable extent. But let me get the situation absolutely straight. Were you the sole individual who knew that the specimen was in that drawer there?'

Dr Lennox considered.

'No, Superintendent,' he said at last. 'There was of course my PA who happened to be present when I put it in that drawer. But, that aside, I still cannot give you such an assurance, not absolutely. For instance, there must be three, four or five people who were working on the substance and who perhaps knew I had taken the specimen away with me. They could have worked out, or simply guessed, it was likely I would have put it in my locked filing cabinet. And, I suppose, one of them might have spoken out of turn.'

'Could you tell me their names, please?' Harriet asked.

For a moment or two Dr Lennox hesitated.

'Very well,' he said then.

He snatched the top sheet from a memo pad on the desk and scribbled the names on it.

'I hope you understand, Superintendent,' he said then, 'that as long as CA 534 is not subjected to a degree of heat it is absolutely inert, and so perfectly safe. I could have happily put it in its protective cardboard box – an empty one from our test tube suppliers – just into a drawer of this desk.'

He gave the wide surface in front of him a proprietorial look.

'I notice the desk is extremely well polished,' Harriet put in. 'That must mean this room is visited by a cleaner. Is that an every day occurrence? Does someone come in here before you arrive?'

'No, no. You mustn't think that, with the importance of the experiments we carry out here, we are not extremely conscious of security. No, the system is that in this office, and in one or two other parts of the house where particularly confidential work is undertaken, every member of the cleaning staff is always under supervision. In the case of my office my personal assistant arrives here well before I do, and opens the door for the cleaner. Subsequently she is watched until she has finished. So, in fact, no one other than myself and my PA can have known for certain that the CA 534 was in that drawer. I was satisfied its security was assured. So should you be, Superintendent.'

Oh, should I?

'If you say so, sir. But I would like all the same to have a word with your PA.'

For the second time she had disconcerted Dr Lennox.

'Very well,' he said at last.

He reached forward and dipped down a switch on the matt black intercom box at the corner of the big desk.

'Come in, would you?'

They waited in silence for a minute or more.

A little to Harriet's surprise the Director's PA proved not to be the pretty young woman she imagined Giles Lennox as gratifying his ego by employing, but a neatly-suited young man, who could equally be described as *pretty*, with well-brushed fair hair over his forehead, big brown eyes, and a come-and-go rosiness of cheek. But someone who was perhaps less likely to be an admiringly submissive office ornament.

'Chris,' Dr Lennox said, 'this is Detective Superintendent Martens. She is here to look into the circumstances of the break-in last night.'

Harriet, who had observed the wince that had crossed the young man's face at that casual 'Chris', gave him a friendly 'good afternoon'.

'You had better take Miss Martens to your own office,

and then see her out,' the Director said. 'I have a good deal of work I should be doing.'

Last strike to you, Harriet said to herself, as the Director stood up and firmly pushed the forced drawer back into its proper place, its dented front obediently straightening itself out with a deep ping.

Chapter Four

Harriet followed the Director's PA – does he prefer to be called full-out *Christopher*, she wondered – along to a much smaller office at the far end of the corridor. Cubbyhole, she thought as she entered, that's the word.

'Take— Take this chair,' Chris, or Christopher, said, hauling from its corner a scuffed leather-seated captain's chair, letting a pile of document wallets slip from it to the floor.

'I— I suppose I ought to introduce myself properly,' he went on, squeezing his way round to his typist-style desk and slipping into the seat behind it. 'I— I'm Christopher Alexander, and, of course, Dr Lennox's PA.'

'Glad to know you, Christopher.'

She saw a small gratified smile appear on the rosy-tinted cheeks.

She took out her notebook.

'But first, may I take your details?'

Christopher's smile disappeared.

'It's just a formality,' she said to him, momentarily wondering why he had been so disconcerted, but deciding this was no more than simple shyness. 'We ask anyone who we're seeking information from.'

A look of relaxation on the cherub face on the other side of the tiny desk, and name and address were trotted out.

'Dr Lennox has been most helpful,' Harriet said. 'But there are one or two points he was unable to assist me with.'

'Well, if I can...'

'Yes. First of all there's the question of who exactly knew where that box of CA 534 had been put for safekeeping. Did you know where it was yourself?'

'Oh, yes. Yes, I was with the Direc— With Dr Lennox when he put it into the filing cabinet. In fact, he asked me to wrap some sticky tape round the box in case the lid somehow came off.'

'I see. And did you watch him after you'd done that? See him lock the drawer?'

'Yes, yes, I did. I saw him take his keys – he has them on a chain, a thin gold chain – from his trouser pocket. It's long enough for him to be able to use the key at the top of the cabinet.'

'Yes, that's all very clear. One has to ask these detailed questions, you know. So, Dr Lennox put the ring of keys back in his trouser pocket? How many others are there on it?'

'Oh, only three or four. I don't think he needs more.'

'I see. And you, do you have a key to the cabinet?'

'I do. Sometimes I have to get out some document Dr Lennox has instructed me to have ready for him.'

'And you have, of course, your own key to his office?'

'Yes. Yes, I have. And naturally I guard it with particular care.'

A touch of his boss's defensiveness rubbing off?

'I'm glad to hear that,' she said placatingly. 'So – am I right? – it was you who actually discovered that the break-in had occurred? When you went – with the cleaning lady, was it? – into Dr Lennox's room at an early hour this morning?'

'Yes. Yes, that was it. And as soon as I saw that drawer wide open and the dent in its front I guessed what must have happened. So I'm afraid I bundled the cleaning lady out of the room straight away, and then I rang Dr Lennox at home. He got here in a few minutes. He doesn't live far away, although he sometimes makes use of the bedroom next to his office, if he's been working very late for instance.'

'That was smart work on your part,' Harriet said, mentally recording that no doubt his *bundling out* of the cleaning lady accounted for the untidiness in the Director's bedroom.

'Well, I'd realised at once what sort of a disaster it would be if anybody got to hear the CA 534 had been stolen. It could wipe out in hours acres and acres of the countryside, you know. And, even worse than that, huge tracts of land could be devastated if the thieves were able to manufacture more from that small specimen. Something that's not too difficult to do, in fact.'

'Could you clarify that for me,' Harriet jumped in. 'Dr Lennox told me CA 534 needed *a degree of heat* to become active. Is that so?'

'Yes, yes, it is. He remarked on it when he was putting the box into the secure cabinet.'

'Or the not-so secure,' Harriet commented with a smile.

No harm in ranging herself on the young man's side against the dictatorial Director.

For a moment it looked as if this little snide comment had had the wrong effect. Christopher seemed distinctly disconcerted. But a moment later the tiny act of resistance was explained.

'You're right, of course,' Christopher said. 'The cabinet turned out not to be totally secure. But then who would expect it to be attacked with a crowbar? If that was what was used. It was only secure enough just to keep any prying eyes from seeing documents they weren't meant to.'

'Yes, of course,' Harriet said. 'But I was asking you about heating the CA 534. How much heat would be necessary?'

'Oh, not much, as I've gathered. Perhaps just exposure to an electric fire, something of that sort. And it would remain active as long as it retained that heat.'

'I see. And would someone, say, with a smattering of scientific knowledge be able to tell, or to guess, that?'

'Yes. Yes, I think they would. Almost anybody with an A-level in chemistry would.'

Yes, Harriet thought, this young man, scared stiff of the Director though he plainly is, is no simpleton.

'Right,' she said, 'tell me more about the box it was in. How big is it? Come to that, how safe is it from being accidentally damaged?'

'Oh, it's perfectly safe. If you're able to retrieve it before the thieves use it, or try to sell it, if that's what they have in mind, then no harm will be done. And, as to its size, it's not very large. The CA 534 itself was in a standard test tube, though one made of specially treated strong glass. It's just a few millilitres of a dark yellow oily liquid, and the box is one that usually holds ten new test tubes. It's about two-hundred millimetres by a hundred, and, say, fifty millimetres deep.'

'Tell me in inches,' Harriet said, with an inward smile at young Christopher showing-off his scientific credentials, such as they were.

He had to calculate for a moment.

'Oh, say about – er – eight inches by four and a couple of inches deep, bit less perhaps.'

'As small as that? And the single tube in it is capable of doing as much damage as you've indicated?'

'Oh, yes, it is. I've seen it at work. The Director conducted a very small experiment, on a specially isolated patch of lawn in the grounds here.'

'And...?'

'Well, I'll tell you what I actually saw. The Director put just two drops of the liquid, pre-heated, down on that small square of grass, and, as soon as they came in contact with the single blade he'd put them on they started to multiply at an extraordinary rate. It's because they feed on chlorophyll. That's the principle behind all the herbicides we've been experimenting with, actually. But, and this is the thing, in almost a minute all the grass in that patch simply disappeared. It was literally eaten up, to the last possible trace.'

For the first time the true extent of the hovering threat made itself clear to Harriet. She felt a rising tide of deep coldness move inside her.

Then another thought came.

Yes, thanks to the vaguer threat hanging over the whole country, post-Hasselburg, it's now been left entirely to me to see how that cardboard box with the single test tube of oily yellow destructor in it can be recovered. It's been left to me.

And then, despite herself, she thought, too, of the personal threat hanging over her and John. Malcolm. Is he, even at this instant, surrendering to the wounds he suffered from that booby-trap explosion?

But, no, I must thrust that aside. All my effort must be directed to countering, if I can, if I possibly can, the more immediate threat.

One small line to follow came back into her mind.

'Tell me,' she said to Christopher. 'Does the name Wichmann, Professor Wichmann, mean anything to you?'

She saw a look of mild astonishment, appear on the pretty face in front of her.

'Professor Wichmann? Do you mean the former Professor of German Studies at Birchester University?'

'I do.'

'Well, yes. Yes, his name does mean something to me, quite a lot even.'

A prick of hope lit up in her. Have I hit straight away on something that's going to lead somewhere? Has the man that MI5, or whoever the Faceless Ones were, suggested to the Chief Constable as possibly behind the theft here, had some contact with the Institute Director's personal assistant? If so...

'What does Professor Wichmann mean to you then? What exactly?'

To her complete surprise Christopher smiled, warmly.

'Well,' he said, 'I read German under him. He— He was a great influence on me really. I mean, I had only opted for a degree in German because at school I happened to have done better at that than French. But when he began to teach me I really discovered what a wealth of stuff there was in German literature. Marvellous stuff. I was—'

He came to a full halt.

'Yes? You were...?'

A deep blush, and a rather strangulated cough.

'Well, you see, when I was in my final year at the university there was some talk, if my degree turned out to be a first as people thought it would, of going on to do a DLitt on a writer called Richter, a very interesting man, though not as well known outside Germany as he ought to be.'

'And...?'

'And, well, in the end I decided not to go for it. I...er... Well, I decided I'd prefer to have a straight job. That's when I got this one. The Director, Dr Lennox, was sort of impressed with my degree. It was a first, actually.'

'But you opted for a regular job rather than the academic life?'

Christopher seemed to jump at this.

'Yes. Yes, that was it. A job. I wanted a proper job. And actually it's a pretty good one. Responsible— Well, quite responsible. And it's very interesting. I've been here two years now, and I suppose eventually, when I feel the time's...er...ripe, I could go on to better things. Science Administration, you know.'

Not a very self-confident young man, Harriet registered.

'Well, good luck,' she said. 'And is that the full extent of your connection with Professor Wichmann? Or are you in contact with him still?'

There might still be something here. If this young man has perhaps been talking about the work here more than he should... And Wichmann, on some list of people to be kept an eye on which the Faceless Ones have, just might have learnt from Christopher about the possibilities of CA 534...

'In contact?' Chris answered. 'Well, no, not really. I do meet him occasionally. If, as I sometimes like to do, I go to a public lecture at the university, on something that particularly interests me, I may chance to see him there, and we chat. I still really admire him, you know.'

Admire him? And do what he asks of you? Even something you know you should not? It could be. Look how he's under the thumb of Dr bloody Lennox, for example. Someone easily controlled. And, possibly, lying to me as he sits squeezed up there behind that wretched desk.

'So Professor Wichmann is still teaching at the university?'

'Well, no. No, he retired the year after I left. But they made him a professor emeritus. He's a really distinguished figure in the academic world.'

'And he still lives in Birchester?'

'Yes, he does. He has, or he did have – I don't know if he's moved now that he's retired – a flat in a little street just off University Boulevard. I used to go there for— Well, for extra tuition. He— Well, actually, he had great hopes for me. The DLitt, you know. So, yes, it's in Bulstrode Road. Rather a poky place, actually. I can't remember the number, but it's above a greengrocer's shop.'

Clam up here. Clam up quick. Don't want him somehow mentioning to Wichmann that I'm interested.

Hastily she moved back to the circumstances of the break-in.

'Now, there's something else you could perhaps tell me.'

'Yes?'

'It's about a story that appeared in the *Evening Star* a few weeks ago. Dr Lennox mentioned it to me just now. He said someone here at the Institute may have spoken out of turn to some reporter or other from the *Star*, about the original discovery of – what was it? – CA 490?'

'No, 491. That was our first full success.'

'Thank you. CA 491. I was wondering, have you any idea who could have spoken to—' A sudden recall. 'To, yes, Tim Patterson of the *Star*. That story was a scoop of his, as I remember. I know the fellow, never short of an exclusive story, though not always one that proves to be strictly accurate.'

'And you're wondering who it was here who talked to him about CA 491? You think they might have spoken to someone else, about CA 534?'

'I wondered, yes.'

'Well, I think I can set your mind at rest there. After that story in the *Star* about CA 491 the Director asked me to make some discreet inquiries, and I was able to put my finger on the culprit. I'm sorry that I was, as a matter of fact.'

'Oh. Why?'

'The chap got the push. That very day.'

'I see. But— But, yes, could he have been aggrieved over that? I imagine Dr Lennox would not be too kind about sacking him.'

'I know what you mean. But, no. I actually went to see the fellow to sort of apologise – I won't tell you his name – and I learnt that he was heading straight off to Australia, he knew of a job there that was his for the asking. So I really don't think he could have anything to do with this business.'

She wondered whether to extract the name of Tim Patterson's informant from this timid and confused young man. But decided not to press him. The chap had apparently gone to Australia, and it was worth keeping Christopher on her side.

'Yes, you're almost certainly right,' she said. 'But can you prepare for me a list of all the employees here, right down to, yes, that cleaning lady. And I don't think I need keep you any longer. Here's my card, if you'd tell me when you've got the list ready. But now, no doubt, Dr Lennox will have things he wants you to do.'

Christopher's pink cheeks paled.

'Oh, gosh, yes. Yes, there's the documents he asked for yesterday.'

Harriet drove directly to University Boulevard. It did not take her long, cruising down it, to find Bulstrode Road, and not much longer to spot half-way along a display of vegetables on the pavement outside a greengrocer's shop.

She parked a short distance further on.

No sense in giving any warning to a man who, if he is in

the flat above the shop, may be sitting with that container of ultra-potent herbicide concealed somewhere on the premises, going over and over in his mind the circumstances of the break-in at Heronsgate House and whether anything about them might lead to him.

She strolled back past the shop, giving a casual appraising glance to its neatly arranged boxes of apples, oranges and pretty side-by-side bunches of green grapes and red. She saw that the way to the flat above must be somewhere at the rear. There were no stairs in the dark depths at the back.

Turning, she found, some fifty yards along the terrace, a narrow passage leading to an alleyway behind. She made her way down it and soon worked out which building must be the greengrocer's. There was a small yard with, under a sloping roof, piled sacks of potatoes, at a guess. And to one side a flight of iron steps led up to a blue door, much faded, with a tinny-looking chrome letterbox at its centre.

With some caution, she climbed up and pressed the button on the little bell-push precariously attached to the door jamb.

A crackly buzz from inside came clearly to her ears.

But nothing else.

The aged professor of German sitting crouched there in fear? Or innocently asleep in his armchair, knowing nothing of any break-in at Heronsgate House?

She buzzed again, and for good measure gave the tinny knocker on the letterbox a long repeated tapping.

Still nothing.

She turned and looked down into the little yard below and then out into what she could see beyond the back wall. Nothing. Nobody.

She dropped to her knees and pushed open with her fingers, wide as she could, the flap of the letterbox. She peered through. But she was able to see almost nothing.

Another quick glance behind her, and then she put her mouth close up to the open flap.

'Hello!' she called.

She listened. No response.

'Hello! Hello!'

Still nothing.

Last try.

'Mr Wichmann! Mr Wichmann! Hello, hello!'

She gave it as long as a count of one hundred. Then she abandoned it.

Rubbing her knees where the iron grating had bitten into them, she made her way down, crossed the earthy-smelling yard with its stored potatoes, and made her way back round into Bulstrode Road and along again to the greengrocer's.

Its proprietor, she saw, was standing now in his doorway, looking out at the world, an Indian or Pakistani, comfortably chubby.

'Good morning,' she said.

'Madam, good morning. There is something I can supply? Today I am having some very fine oranges, and grapes also. Very good, nothing of seeds.'

'No. No, thank you. Or, perhaps later. But I really wanted to ask you about the man who lives in the flat above you. Professor Wichmann.'

'Ah, yes, very fine gentleman.'

'He doesn't seem to be there. Do you know if he's out?'

'Yes, yes. He has gone to university library. He was telling. Always when he is going out, if I am here, he is mentioning. Very good. When you are old, that is always best.'

'Yes. Yes, you're right. A sensible precaution. So you think I could find him at the university? In the library there?'

'Oh, it is yes and no also. He would go for shopping also.'

Harriet had to admit defeat. Try later in the day.

She thanked – she looked up at the fascia above – Mr Chaudhuri, bought a bunch of his nothing-of-seeds grapes, and, back in the car, considered what her next step should be.

Precious little progress so far. All right, I've got the description of the intruders which those two security idiots produced. But they were fuzzy about it all, to say the least. Get hold of them again? Certainly should at some point. Something not quite right there. But seeing them again as soon as this isn't going to produce anything more. They'll have to stew.

There's something else too, scratching at a corner of my mind. About Christopher Alexander, I think. Was there a moment when he seemed more than usually unsure? When he may have been boxing clever somehow?

But she could pin nothing down. Abruptly an idea for a new approach came to her.

Those stories in the *Star* about the Heronsgate Institute, surely their chief crime reporter so-called, Tim Patterson, must know a good deal about the place. Worth picking his brains, old adversary from press conferences though he is?

Yes, a word with him. The horse's mouth. If a vicious one.

But...

But how to approach him? At all costs I mustn't give him the least hint of the theft of the CA 534.

By the time she had arrived at the *Star* office she felt she had solved the problem. Brushing aside Tim Patterson's pretty perfunctory condolences – Hologram Harriet fully in control – she said, 'I expect you're surprised to find me here. But I've come to satisfy something nagging at me. When we were down in London on Tuesday, seeing our injured son, as we came out of St Mary's Hospital late at night, my husband spotted an early copy of the *Banner* with a headline saying *PC Twins in Bomb Blast*. Seeing it suddenly like that hurt me rather, to tell the truth, and ever since I've been puzzling myself as to how they knew so quickly down there that the boys were twins. So, forgive me, but I've come to the experts for an answer.'

Then, to her astonishment, she saw something like a blush appear on Tim Patterson's usually intently pale face.

'I— I—' he stammered. 'Well, I can explain that myself actually. You see, I'm the stringer here for the *Banner*, and, whenever there's a story with a Birchester angle, it's sort of my duty to phone it in to them.'

'Oh, well,' Hologram Harriet said coolly, 'that accounts for it.'

But Real Harriet, almost at the surface, had other thoughts.

So that's how that bloody paper got that headline. A cheap thrill for its readers. And never mind my misery. Our misery.

Hologram Harriet, however, was still well in charge.

'Look,' she said, 'it must be past opening time now, so come for a drink. Show there's no ill-feeling.'

She saw a look of faint disbelief on Tim Patterson's face, but he got to his feet and accompanied her to a quiet pub, The Leather Bottle, not far away.

There, ordering a Guinness for him – she remembered he called that *a reporter's drink* – and a lager for herself, plus a sandwich when she realised she had eaten nothing since a barely tasted breakfast, she began cautiously to approach finding out how much poke-nose Patterson knew about Heronsgate House.

But she had not got far when her mobile squeaked out.

'Excuse me, a second.'

Then to the mobile 'Yes?'

'It's John, darling. I've just heard from St Mary's. Malcolm's recovered consciousness. He's very weak, of course, and they suggest it would be best if we waited till tomorrow before going down to see him in case it's all too much for him.'

'Yes. Yes, I understand what they're saying, but tomorrow...'

'I know what you mean. But we must accept their advice, at least to some extent. But we could, I think, go late this evening, if it's OK. Apparently all he's been able to do so far is mutter a few words, *Where am I? What happened?*

That sort of thing. And beyond telling him where he was and that he was in good hands, that's all they thought they should say. For the time being at least.'

'Yes, of course. But, John, it's wonderful. Wonderful, isn't it? And we could always ring and ask if we can come tonight, couldn't we?'

'We could, if all still goes well, yes. We'll talk this evening. And there'll be something else to discuss, actually. The people at St Mary's want to know when we're going to have Graham's funeral. They were very good about it, but I think they're anxious to keep the maximum amount of space in the mortuary there. In case of what they call *a major incident.*'

Her thoughts whirled. Funeral, funeral. Yes, there'll have to be one. A funeral for the shattered remains. A coffin, like a box of butcher's waste. And Malcolm. The hospital's more optimistic, but how long will it be before he's on his feet, if he ever is. Should we delay a funeral? God, I don't know. I can't think. We've neither of us given it a thought. Unless John has had it in his head. But I haven't. I haven't at all.

'But, you?' John's voice came in her ear. 'How did your interview with the formidable Mr Brown go?'

'I'll tell you tonight. Can't talk at present.'

She cut the call.

'That was about your son?' Tim Patterson asked. 'The one in hospital? I couldn't help hearing. It sounded like good news.'

'It was. Malcolm's recovered consciousness, thank God.'

'Oh, that's good. Very good.'

For a moment she warmed to him. But then she caught a tiny hint of calculation in his eyes and realised that what he was really thinking was *bit of a story here, must get back to the office, make the final edition.*

All right, I'm going to use this damn fellow.

'I've been thinking recently,' she said, 'about the piece you wrote the other day on that runaway herbicide they contrived to manufacture at Heronsgate House. I expect the stuff's been destroyed now, but it has occurred to me – You know I'm in charge of Greater Birchester Police terrorist precautions – that if something like that got into the hands of any terrorist organisation it might prove as much of a threat as whatever explosives they normally acquire.'

She saw Tim Patterson's eyes light up. Some bigger story here?

'So I was wondering how you got hold of your facts about that herbicide going critical, if that's the right expression. I mean, if you could get to know about something at Heronsgate House which they wanted kept strictly confidential, perhaps some terrorist outfit could do the same?'

A bit flimsy, she thought. But will it...?

It did.

'So your anti-terrorist precautions extend even to a place like the Heronsgate Institute?' Tim asked, with ill-concealed eagerness.

'Oh, yes. Indeed they do. Or they're going to very soon.'

'And it'd help you if you learnt the secret of the *Star* crime correspondent's methods?'

'It very well might, and I'd be grateful.'

'OK. Well, basically it's very simple. What you do is make sure you've got as many contacts, up and down the city, as you can possibly get. It involves, I'm sorry to say, more than a little imbibing of alcohol. But one must suffer in a good cause.'

He gave a grin.

An unpleasant grin, Harriet thought. More of a smirk.

'And you found a contact at Heronsgate House?' she asked.

'Chap called Oliphant, actually. Recently sacked, I'm sorry to say. And in Australia now, poor sod.'

Damn. Trail ending at something I've already found out.

'So you don't actually know now anything at all about

the set-up at Heronsgate House?' she said, provocatively.

Tim Patterson sat up straighter.

'Oh, don't I? You mustn't think when I'm on to something that, if one door shuts, I don't get my foot in at another. No, I'm happy to say I go drinking from time to time now with a chap who's actually PA to the Director there. Name of Chris Alexander.'

Chris to you as well as to his boss. I bet he doesn't like that, poor Christopher.

But Tim Patterson was happily boasting on.

'Got to know him through a girlfriend of mine who works on the women's page at the *Chronicle*, Maggie Quirke. Ex-girlfriend, I should say. I...er...let Chris take her over. I was getting tired of her, tell the truth. Very fanciable, wonderful body – she's a marathon runner – big white-teeth smile and all that. But, alas, not much of an athlete in bed. So I passed her on. Pretended to Chris he stole her off me. He's so unsure of himself, it isn't true. That's how one gets a good contact.'

Another smirk of a smile.

So, yes, Harriet thought, I was right to feel something was not hundred per cent kosher when I was talking to Christopher. He must have been wondering all along if he'd said more than he should to this nasty piece of work here.

'I never realised the lengths someone like you has to go to,' she said, heading Tim off from things it was better he should have no idea of. 'I'm impressed, really. I'm surprised you haven't got yourself down to Fleet Street.'

Compliment received, with evident pleasure.

'Oh, I could get a job down there, when I'm ready. But there's a lot to be said for being a big fish in a small pond, you know. For instance, I dare say you remember my exclusive about that mad outfit called WAGI?'

'Waggy? I don't think...'

'Surely you must remember. It was a running story for weeks. Even you in the police became part of it.'

'I'm sorry. But—' She momentarily choked, recovered

herself. 'But, that bomb, in London, has blotted out a lot I should remember.'

Is it worth having lied to this obnoxious sod, or lied with the truth, just so as to learn something that's pretty unlikely to be any use to me?

Then, yes, she answered. Anything that gets me half an inch nearer finding out where that CA 534 is must be worthwhile. A police officer's duty.

'So what was this story – something waggy? – you got hold of?'

'My waggy story, as you kindly put it. Well, waggy is— I'd better spell it out. It's W-A-G-I, Women Against Genetic Interference. They began as a little female talk-shop somewhere out in Boreham and then they spread to all Birchester and, they like to claim, to all sorts of other places.'

'Yes, now you say that, I do recall them. Didn't we have to bring them up to the magistrates' court for destroying a crop of GM maize?'

'You've got it. And why did they land up in the dock, and lucky to get away with just being fined? Because Tim Patterson of the *Star* had a contact – my disappointing girlfriend, actually – who belonged to WAGI. Hey, and you know what? A relation of your husband's another member, up before the beak too.'

Tim Patterson of the *Star* broke into honking laughter.

Harriet, pricked with rage at last, downed the lager she had ordered and stood up.

'Well, you've been a help, Tim,' she said. 'Thank you.'

And, leaving him to make what he could of that, she made her way out.

In the car she looked at her watch. Yes, a good deal of time gone by since Professor Wichmann had set off, first for the university library then, as helpful Mr Chaudhuri had put it, 'for shopping'. So back to Bulstrode Road and the man the Faceless Ones had put their finger on. And I must remember, too, to ask John about that relative of his.

Chapter Five

'He was coming back,' Mr Chaudhuri called out, as he put a bag of his *very fine* oranges into a housewife's shopping trolley.

Giving him a grateful wave, Harriet hurried away to the passage leading to the alleyway at the rear of the neat terraces of Bulstrode Road. In less than two minutes she had put her finger on the little white button crazily set in the narrow door jamb. Its crackly buzz came to her ears.

But now another sound came from inside. Ponderous footsteps.

Then the blue door was drawn fully back.

Harriet saw a man, perhaps in his eighties, white hair fluffy round a ruddy, bald dome of a head, a generous white moustache failing to conceal a long row of china-white false teeth, a paunch well protected by a tobacco-coloured cardigan. But, however telling of the latter years all this was, the two blue eyes looking back at her were twinklingly alive.

She had prepared her opening words, bouncing them out before the old professor had any chance to speak himself.

'Mr Wichmann? Police.'

But, if she had hoped the brutal announcement would go to the core of the man the Faceless Ones had suggested as being behind the theft at Heronsgate House, she was to be disappointed. He appeared, at once, to be a little disconcerted, but no more than that.

So, a tougher proposition than his mild appearance might suggest? Or someone altogether innocent?

'The police?' he said now.

He produced a plainly cheerful smile, the serried ranks of paint-white teeth briefly showing.

'What is it I have done? Have I been driving the car I do not possess at a speed in excess of two hundred miles per hour? Or has Mr Chaudhuri down below denounced me for stealing from him one apple?'

Harriet, producing her warrant card, returned smile for smile.

Plainly, if the Faceless Ones were right about the old man, it was going to be a long and difficult business getting to the truth of him.

'No, sir,' she replied. 'Detective Superintendent Martens isn't here dangling a pair of handcuffs. But may I come in and tell you what is my reason for calling?'

'Yes, yes. Come in, come in. My little home.'

He turned and, padding along in front of her, led her into his sitting-room or study.

She took the quick survey she made, almost without thinking, on entering anywhere on inquiries. Yes, there was the armchair she had earlier envisaged Professor Wichmann as dozing in. It was tall-backed with draughts-protecting wings and covered in some tan-coloured material, now glistening in patches with long years of use. There was an electric fire in the fireplace, both its two bars issuing heat on this unpleasantly chilly day. On the floor a patterned carpet, a little too big for the area it covered, showed patches almost worn down to the backing threads. There was a dark-stained desk, big – too big again for the little room – and heaped with books and papers. Down beside it, she saw an uncovered typewriter, of a make that might have been produced as long as fifty years ago. And on every available space round the walls there were bookshelves crammed higgledy-piggledy with academic-looking volumes.

Portrait of the Professor.

But, if the Faceless Ones had any hard evidence for pointing to him, might it be Portrait of the Sleeper Spy?

Take another unexpected swing at him? Why not? He may have parried that single word *Police* I shot out, but a second such low blow may penetrate his defences. If there are defences for him to have.

'Professor Wichmann,' she said, 'what do you know

about Heronsgate House?'

A quietly perplexed frown the only reaction.

But then, suddenly, a sharp look in those blue eyes.

'Ah, yes. Yes, that is where a young protégé of mine is now working.'

So my second shock as unproductive as the first.

Professor Wichmann, with a long breathy sigh, dropped into his battered armchair, vaguely indicating to Harriet a sturdy cushioned one by the desk.

'Yes,' he said, 'that boy is now personal assistant to the Director at that place, Heronsgate House, and he should not be. He should be here, here at the university, working on his thesis on Jean Paul.'

Harriet was quick.

That was not been the name of the German writer Christopher Alexander had said he had decided not to study. A chink? A chink in a prepared story of some sort?

'Jean Paul?'

Professor Wichmann gave her a smile, a roguish glint from the china teeth.

'Ah, yes,' he said, 'I would not expect an English police lady, even of high rank, to know Jean Paul, though his is a name to be found in the works of the greatest of all writers of crime stories.'

'Conan Doyle? Sherlock Holmes?'

'Good, good. But, nevertheless, you do not remember the name Jean Paul?'

Harriet grinned, a little sheepishly.

'Well, I have to say that it's my husband who's the really keen reader of the Holmes stories.'

'Yes, yes. They are often preferred by what I must not nowadays speak of as the stronger sex. So, let me tell you. In the course of his investigation of the case of *The Sign of Four*, Sherlock Holmes, reflecting, as I remember, on the beauty of the day's dawn, mentions Jean Paul, as Jean Paul Richter was commonly called in those days.'

Another tenuous threat falling away to nothing. Harriet

felt almost inclined to laugh.

'Ah, yes,' she said, 'this morning when I was making some inquiries at Heronsgate House your protégé, as you called him, Christopher Alexander, told me he had once contemplated doing a DLitt on, yes, Richter. But, he said, he had decided to take a job instead.'

'Yes, yes,' the old man opposite her sighed. 'The silly unsure-of-himself boy. I had hoped... I thought once that he would even become my successor here at the university, that my work, such as it was, would still be kept alive. But, no. It was not to be. A loss to scholarship, even a considerable loss.'

But is Christopher, Harriet asked herself now, a young man who bitterly regrets that decision of his, with perhaps its promise of eventual academic fame. And has he – can it be? – taken a sort of revenge on his present occupation by betraying the Director's secret. But to whom? To someone, or some group, who wanted to get their hands on a weapon as threatening as CA 534? And who had swiftly acted on the information they had acquired?

On the other hand, it could be that the Faceless Ones have got their beady eyes to some purpose on— On this pleasant old professor of German, sitting there in that dilapidated but comfortable chair. So, yes, let's try another shock-tactics blow.

'Professor, does it surprise you to be told that I am here because I have been given your name by the British secret services?'

It did surprise the old man. That was clearly evident. But it was as evident that it had not actually shocked him.

'Well,' he said at last. 'Well, I am, I must confess, not entirely surprised by that. You know, I spent the early years of my life prepared at every moment to hear some such news as you have given me. Not that the British secret service was interested in a seventeen-year-old German boy, but that the Gestapo had me, and more credibly my father, in their sights.'

The Gestapo. Into Harriet's head there came thoughts and memories culled from dozens of films and television thrillers she had seen, even from television comedies. In all of them, seriously or comically, the Gestapo meant an ever-lurking threat of sudden arrest, of the concentration camp, of torture possibly, of soon-to-come death. And, no doubt, this old man, that once seventeen-year-old youth, had been under such a threat.

'So,' she said, 'you were living in Germany in the days shortly before the Second World War?'

'Yes, yes. In those terrible times. My father, who was a distinguished historian, had married a Jewish lady, and, although she died when I was no more than five years old, the taint was seen always to be there. We, father and son, were conscious every day that the knock might come at the door. So, you can see how still, at the back of my mind, I have a fear. No, it is less than that. I have a dislike of feeling that I'm being watched.'

'Yes. Yes, I can understand that.'

'Ah,' Professor Wichmann said, with that momentary teasingness Harriet was beginning to expect from him, the gentle rib-poking perhaps of a professor with students he liked, 'but do you understand this? It is something I learnt in those days in Germany. There are people also who do like to think they are being watched, who like feeling threatened?'

Harriet thought.

'No,' she admitted at last. 'I've always known there are areas of the human psyche that I cannot get any grasp on, neither sympathy nor revulsion. But if you tell me there are people of that sort, I will believe you.'

Then, abruptly, she thought of Christopher Alexander again. Was he one such? Perhaps this was why Professor Wichmann had taken such an interest in him. And perhaps, too, that was the hidden reason why he might have told someone – but who? – where Dr Lennox had hidden the potentially devastating CA 534.

But Professor Wichmann was going on.

'For a long while my father had attempted to leave Germany. Something by no means as easy to do then as your happy holiday-maker of today would believe. But at last he succeeded, and of course he brought me with him. Here to England. And for him to imprisonment, or internment as they politely called it.'

A teasing smile.

'But for me, seen as too young, there was, yes, freedom. If, as it now seems from what you have just told me, freedom under licence, so to speak, with my name for ever inscribed on some Secret Service list. But it was, nevertheless, freedom, freedom to study what I wished. Even, in wartime, to study the literature of the enemy country where I had been born. The literature that I loved.'

Had he blinked away a tear?

'And you, unlike Christopher Alexander, did go on to higher studies? And to a lectureship, or whatever? And eventually to becoming Professor of German Studies at Birchester University?'

'Yes, yes. Even to finding myself Emeritus Professor, something that makes me, however unworthily, proud. And to having, so far from always fearing that knock on the door, become one who, again in Sir Arthur Conan Doyle's words, believes in *the magnificent fair play of the British police*. All that is the debt I owe to this country, this peaceful country, of which I have long been a citizen.'

Harriet, abruptly finding back in her consciousness the violence that had shattered her two sons, uttered an incredulous, 'Peaceful?'

'Ah, yes,' Professor Wichmann replied. 'Yes, I can see that you— But, stop. Stop. Yes, did you say your name was Martens? Are you – can it be that you are the lady – you have some different married name? – whose twin sons, young police officers, have been – I was reading just this morning in the *Birchester Chronicle* – victims of a terrible bomb outrage?'

'Yes. Yes, I'm afraid that's so.'

'But— But how does it come about then that you are here, on duty, making some unimportant inquiries?'

Harriet managed some sort of a smile, or mirthless grin.

'That's because this country is at this time not any sort of a peaceful place,' she said. 'I see you have no television. But you must have read in the *Chronicle* about worse outrages than the attack on my sons.'

'All those deaths just a few days ago, the EuroVin festival, yes. But Hasselburg is not in England.'

'No, but at any moment some English city, Birchester perhaps, may become another Hasselburg.'

'Yes. Yes, that is true. You do well to remind me. Yet I can still think of this country as peaceful. It has been so for me, for many years. I have been able to go walking in the beautiful countryside. The beautiful and peaceful countryside. Not perhaps, to my mind, quite as beautiful as the *Schwartzwald*, the Black Forest, where I used to go walking with my father long ago, but beautiful enough, the Lake District, the moors of Yorkshire, Exmoor, Dartmoor, the Scottish Highlands. Beautiful, beautiful and, yes, peaceful.'

The hymn of praise had given Harriet time to recover herself.

'Yes,' she said, 'I know what you mean. Britain was beautiful and peaceful once.'

Professor Wichmann shook his head.

'No, no, my dear. You should not make that mistake. You are dreaming, dreaming of something that has never really existed. Yes, I have had delightful holidays walking in all those places, and, yes, peace, a sort of peace, entered my soul then. But the reality was there all the time. Was there ever a period here, has there ever been a time in the world, when all was truly peaceful? No. No, there has not. Wars have been fought in the beautiful places of Britain, plagues have killed their thousands here and everywhere, and surely you have read of the great Lisbon earthquake of 1755, which gave philosophers all over the civilised world so much to think about and was seen as such a challenge to Voltaire's saying that this is the best of all possible worlds.'

You're far beyond me now Professor, Harriet thought.

But he had one more word for her yet.

'Yes, my dear, there is always threat hanging above us, truly hanging above us. Remember all those pictures you have seen of the mushroom clouds of nuclear bomb tests.'

Harriet thought for a moment.

'All right,' she said then. 'Of course I still have that image somewhere in my mind. But, do you know, it doesn't make me feel threatened. I suppose it did when I first saw it, when we all first saw it. But it's extraordinary how quickly it ceased to have the effect it should have done. My husband has a quotation that explains it, I think. TS Eliot, *human kind cannot bear very much reality.*'

A quite unexpected smile appeared then on Professor Wichmann's face, lined-up china-white teeth flashing.

'Yes, your husband is right. But there is something else also. Something we should not forget. There has always been, among all the threats, hope. The hope that things will be better one day. It has been, even, the everyday, every morning, hope that – you will laugh at me, I think – that the postman will bring a letter and in it there will be good news.'

And can this, Harriet found herself thinking, be the man behind the theft of the ultra-dangerous CA 534, rather than the easily-led, perhaps delighting in being under a threat, Christopher Alexander? Is this nice man holding a terrible threat over all the – yes, peaceful – countryside from Land's End to John o' Groats?

Chapter Six

Then despair struck. Harriet had left Professor Wichmann's flat, with its faint scent of vegetables rising up from the greengrocer's below, going over in her mind all that she had learnt there. The shadowy evidence for either the professor himself or his protégé, Christopher Alexander, being behind the break-in at Heronsgate House. But hardly had she gone out of the shop's cramped back-yard when, for some reason or none, the thought of Malcolm came thunderbolting into her head, Malcolm lying there in St Mary's suffering from appalling injuries. Of Malcolm, perhaps just beginning to realise that his twin, whose life had intertwined with his own for all the twenty years of their existence, was dead.

The thick misery that had invaded every part of her when, with that out-of-the-blue phone call, she had learnt what had happened to the twins, came swirling and eddying back. There, in the cobbled alleyway behind the neat houses of Bulstrode Road, she stood unable to advance by so much as another step.

Graham. Graham dead. Blown to pieces in some deliberate act. And Malcolm, yes, alive and able to speak now, but terribly, horribly injured. My two sons, who had so pleased me, so much endorsed my life by choosing to go into the profession I myself chose long ago. And both out of it now. Graham dead and Malcolm unlikely ever to be able to work as a police officer again.

At length, Hologram Harriet, seemingly there once more, took over.

God, yes, what time is it? We were going to try to see Malcolm tonight.

The Hologram, glancing at her watch, was unable to read it until the tears which had been ready to pour down dried at her eyelids.

Five minutes to five. And I've gone all through this day

scarcely having eaten anything, except that foul pub sandwich which I hardly touched.

Right then, home. Go to the car, get in it and drive home, where I shall cook myself whatever I find in the fridge and eat it, nice or nasty.

And at home she at once heard John, equally having quit his desk early, greet her.

'Jesus, darling, you look all-in.'

She managed a sort of smile.

'Well, I am pretty much bushed. I've had a busy day. Mr Brown allocated me a task. It involved interview after interview, so much so that I forgot to get myself any lunch.'

'Well, well. Was this some sort of punishment for what you failed to say in your TV appearance?'

'Oh, no. Far from it. Mr Brown actually congratulated me on what I came out with, though he swore I was to tell no one. No trouble there.'

'But then, as you hinted, you were given some work? I'm surprised, I must say.'

'So was I, to begin with. But Mr Brown pointed out to me that, the security situation being what it is, the whole of Greater Birchester Police, more or less, is on anti-terrorist duties. And then he told me that there had been a break-in at that place, Heronsgate House, and that— Of course, I'm not meant to be telling you any of this but, of course, I am. A specimen, the only remaining one, of that hyperactive herbicide they accidentally brought into existence has been stolen. A gang, if that's what they should be called, broke in there last night and apparently went straight up to the Director's office, where he had chosen to hide the one specimen he had kept, despite an instruction to destroy all the runaway stuff. Mr Brown suggested it would be good for me, although I was entitled to a period of leave, to work. And that's what I've been doing ever since, working. Working flat-out. And all in a sort of vacuum.'

'Well, for God's sake, sit down. Sit down, and I'll fetch you a: a drink, and b: some hot soup or something.'

Harriet did as she was told. She felt, in any case, that she could hardly have stood on her feet a moment longer.

And John, she thought after minutes of blankness since he had left the room, John, on my mobile at that pub, The Leather Bottle, told me Malcolm was able to talk. We must find out if we can see him.

But didn't he say, too, that we must think about Graham's funeral? As we have to. There has to be a funeral, and it's up to us, I suppose, to say what sort of funeral it should be, where and when, private or public.

Oh God, I can't do it. I can't. It's too much. Too much for me.

John came back in, a big steaming mug of soup in his hand.

'Get yourself outside this. And I'll fix you a whisky.'

Obediently Harriet took the mug, but found it too hot to drink from. In a minute or two John, at the little fridge where they kept the drinks, produced the whisky.

Well, he's certainly made it a big one, she thought. And then she swallowed.

She felt the stinging presence of the supermarket whisky, generally drunk doused with ginger ale, flood into her. She took a second big swig and found only a thin amber drain remaining at the bottom of the glass.

'OK,' she said, half-resisting, half-embracing the heady glow that had taken possession of her. 'OK, we have to talk.'

'You're sure?'

'Oh, yes. Yes, I am. But if we leave it much longer I'll be incapable of anything.'

'Take a sip of that soup then. It's only out of a can – mushroom, I think it said – but whatever it is it'll steady you for a little.'

'John, what would I do without you?'

'You'd manage,' he answered with a smile. 'But, all right, let's first decide on a time to go down to Malcolm. What if we set off, let's see, in an hour or so. That should get us to

St Mary's by early evening. I don't suppose it matters much to the nursing staff when we visit. And, if Malcolm's asleep or anything, then, well, we can wait.'

'Yes. Yes, that's easy enough to settle on. But— But, John, didn't you say they wanted at St Mary's to know when the— The funeral...?'

She realised the whisky had ceased to do its work. Looking down at the soup mug beside her, she found a repulsive layer of wrinkles had gathered on its surface.

John's still talking to me.

Must pay attention.

She heaved in a long breath, and found what John was telling her now, apparently, was something new.

'Darling, you're totally exhausted. Let me get you up to bed. Have a sleep for an hour, and if you're fit after that we'll set off. We can talk again in the car.'

She was fit enough, an hour or so later, to get up, wash her face, put on a different suit, and stagger down to the car.

But she was not fit enough to talk as they drove through the cold, clear early Spring evening. Although she did not fall sleep again, she could do no more as the miles on the motorway slipped by than rouse herself occasionally to ask how far they had got. And, in some far part of her mind, she kept puzzling over who it could have been, just twenty-four hours earlier, who had sent those three, four, five ruthless professionals into Heronsgate House and up to the Director's office where they had known exactly how to get hold of the CA 534.

And then, once again, she found they were outside St Mary's, though this time John did not attempt – it must be past nine o'clock, she thought muzzily – to park illegally. Instead, he drove around and around until at last he found a possible space.

As he finally switched off the engine, Harriet found she was all but shaking with a suddenly arrived anger.

Why, why, are stupid regulations preventing us, the parents of a dead son and a terribly injured one, from going straight to his bedside? Malcolm may be on the point of death once more, and this absurd fuss about parking regulations is making it impossible for us to be with him.

'John,' she spat out, 'why the hell are we parked in this godforsaken spot when— When— Oh, God, I don't know what...'

'When, you were going to say,' John answered with a calmness that irritated her even more, 'Malcolm may be on the point of death. But, you know, he won't be, not now. Or, not unless something entirely unexpected has happened. I rang St Mary's from home while you were asleep. You remember I told you as we started off? They said he was still wholly conscious, and asking questions.'

'Oh yes, I remember. Or do I? I don't know. And John...John, has someone told Malcolm about Graham? Did they say on the phone that they had?'

'No. No, they haven't told him. I asked, and they said it might be best if we were the ones to do that.'

'Oh, John. John, how awful. How can— No. No, let's hurry. Hurry.'

She took John's arm, snatched at it, and they set off for the big HM Queen Elizabeth the Queen Mother building deep inside the hospital complex.

When Harriet had seen Malcolm late at night on the day he had been the horribly injured victim of the bomb that had killed his brother she had hardly been able to look at the bandaged body on the other side of the intensive-care ward window, at his nose, mouth and arm, tubes and wires that seemed barely to be supporting life. Now, though he was still in intensive care, she and John had been allowed into the ward.

And the first thing she took in was Malcolm's eyes, dark brown like John's and his brother's, looking up at her, glowing with the understanding of who had come in.

'Malcolm,' she said. 'Well, here you are.'

It was all she could manage.

'How— How's it going?' John put in, almost as tongue-tied.

'OK.'

The word was feebly pronounced, but it came to Harriet as the drawing of a bung from an immense barrel of anxieties. Her words in response poured out.

'Oh, Malcolm, Malcolm, we've been so worried about you. We thought— We thought, well, we couldn't help asking ourselves at every minute whether you, too, were going, like— '

She came to choked halt.

The words she had been about to utter presented themselves in her head as if they were written in bright, pulsing red letters, *you, too, were going, like Graham, to die.*

How— How could I have had on my lips that cruel phrase? How could I have been about to give this son of mine, his head and his arms on top of the coverlet still bandaged, with, hidden below, God knows how many other injuries, how could I have been on the point of blurting out that his brother, his twin, is dead?

Then from the bed came a few more weakly pronounced words.

'It's all ri'. I know. Or— Or I suppose...I must somehow...Graham died, didn't he? When that... He couldn't have sur—' A long patch of silence. ''Vived. He is dead, isn't he?'

'Yes, darling,' she said quickly, before tears came. 'Yes, I'm afraid it's so. That bomb killed him, they believe, instantly.'

'Malcolm,' John said quietly. 'Don't think more about it now. Let it gradually sink in. That's the best way. What you've got to do now is get yourself better again. Just concentrate on that, old chap. Getting better.'

'Yes.'

The word was scarcely audible. The brown eyes slowly drooped closed.

They waited there for a few minutes more, but Malcolm seemed to be solidly asleep.

Eventually John spoke again, his voice barely above a whisper.

'Perhaps we'd better go. Leave him to recover.'

'Yes.'

Once again, passing the reception desk, John spotted a copy of the *Banner*, evidently left there routinely by whoever was accustomed to read the very early edition. For a moment he stood looking down at it indecisively. Then he picked it up and turned it over.

There was a front-page headline *Foreign Bombers Claim Responsibility.*

Harriet watched as, for the second time in such nightmare circumstances, he read, eyes skimming, the text below.

He looked up.

'Apparently,' he said, 'it wasn't al-Qaeda, but some Indian terrorists. They say they're fighting against all forms of Western imperialism, and this is the first warning they're giving that everything Western must be taken out of India. God knows what they can mean by that. The English language? All those British buildings? Hollywood films? They must be mad. Mad.'

'They've killed Graham and made Malcolm into a cripple for life, and they're claiming *responsibility*. What responsibility, I ask you. What is responsible about planting a bomb?'

'God knows. I don't. But— But I suppose we ought to have expected something like that.'

'Yes,' she answered dully.

'But it looks, it really looks, as if Malcolm's going to survive.'

'Yes.'

Suddenly John thrust his face close to hers.

'Is that all you can say? *Yes, Yes* and *Yes?*'

She turned towards him, the anger that had spurted up in her as they had got out of the car, the senseless, ill-directed rage, boiling and bubbling up with renewed force.

'For Christ's sake, what do you expect me to say? What else is there to say but *Yes*? Yes, Malcolm is still alive. But will he be alive tomorrow, or the next day, or next week? For God's sake, that was an intensive care ward we saw him in. Don't you know what that means? It means he's on the edge. On the edge. On the edge of following Graham to death. To death, death, death.'

Then she saw in John's face a red rage, every bit as overwhelming as her own.

'Yes,' he shouted out, oblivious of the man at the desk looking at them both, 'and you know why Malcolm's on the edge of death, why Graham's dead? It's because of you. You. It was you who went on urging them to go into the police. They could have done anything. They were bright, bright boys. They could have been lawyers, top-class civil servants, in business, anything. They could have even be with the Majestic at this moment, have jobs there with plenty of prospects. But no, what did you hammer and hammer at them to be? Police officers. In the danger zone. Every minute of their lives in the danger zone. And you put them there. Yes, you. You.'

She felt as if, in this bright cubicle of light she had been totally, unexpectedly assaulted. A rain of blows from nowhere.

Is he right? she asked herself, cowering from those bludgeon strokes. Has John been harbouring such thoughts all along? And did I in truth force the boys into the Met? Is this all my fault? I did want them to join the service. I did. But— But it's a good job, a necessary job. It is. But did I all the same press them too hard, show them too much how pleased and proud I would be?

She wanted to clutch at something, some corner or projection of the building behind, to stop herself falling.

But she rejected doing so.

No, damn it, he's wrong. John's wrong. And I'm not going to let him ride me down like this.

She straightened up, ready for battle.

And then realised what had happened.

John, my John, is as crushed and beaten down by what I heard on the telephone on Tuesday as I am. But he's fought against it all. Until now. Until he read that piece in the paper, that claiming of responsibility, and thought of Malcolm, lying there above us now, alive but barely able to speak. And it was too much for him. Too much for him, of course.

So what did he do, what could he not stop himself from doing, when I, like a fool, gave way to my feelings of despair and horror? His rage at the senseless thing that happened had to burst out somewhere, and he just attacked the nearest target. Me.

'John,' she said, 'no.'

She took in a long breath.

'No, we must cling together now. For Malcolm's sake, if nothing else. We mustn't let this force us apart. I— I had no idea you were feeling what you were. I thought you felt as I did. I thought you were proud of what the boys had decided to do, something so worthwhile. I never thought...'

She saw the blood was draining from John's cheeks, from his forehead.

'No,' he said with growing leadenness. 'No, I didn't ever think that either. I don't know what came over me just now. Everything I said just formed itself in my mind as I said it. Of course, I never wanted to see the boys sitting there in the Majestic offices somewhere, doing nothing but arrange the fiddling terms of policies. All right, insurance is necessary. We're realising that now after the ruins of Hasselburg, of all the other places in the world that terrorists threaten. And I'm happy I made insurance my career. But, if I'd had any choice when I left university, other than to take the first decently paying job that came up – my mother a widow, don't forget, and a poor one – I'd have almost certainly looked around for a job I could be proud of doing. But I didn't have the time, and I'm glad, enormously glad, that the boys did. And of the choice that they made.'

It was a quiet drive through the cold night back to Birchester. Neither of them spoke much, but they could, it seemed, each feel the warmth that crossed from one to the other. The warmth of steady confidence.

And Harriet, just every now and again, turned her mind to the task the ACC had, so unexpectedly but so sensibly, given to her.

Waking next morning, rather earlier than her usual time, she found that in sleep her subconscious had gone onwards to shift her back into being, not the mother of two bomb-victim young police constables, but a senior officer charged with an important and urgent investigation. She lay there, her mind clicking through the tasks ahead. First, she thought, as she grasped with both hands the top of her separate duvet, ready to push it off – leaving John beside her with twenty snug minutes extra – first it may be most useful to take another look at Christopher Alexander, now that I know more about him.

Night thoughts, dream thoughts, had mysteriously brought Dr Lennox's PA to the forefront of her mind.

There's a lot about him that's still to be discovered. Why, really, did he ditch a highly promising academic career for a spaniel job looking after the Heronsgate Director's trivial wants, keeping his diary, fetching and carrying, escorting visitors like me safely off the premises? All right, he told me he saw a career in science administration before him, and, yes, he indicated he had somehow feared the DLitt examiners he would one day have to argue his case in front of.

So, if, as may be likely, timid, unsure of himself Christopher has managed to get himself a live-in journalist girlfriend, might it not be a good thing to pay him a call, not at Heronsgate House, where presumably he'll be arriving at much about this time to supervise the cleaning lady, but at his new love-nest?

Well, that will have to wait until he's back there.

So, first, go and see Inspector Skelton, Special Branch. He should have been given whatever information it was that caused the Faceless Ones to name Professor Wichmann. Skelton, a curious, reticent, buried-in-himself man, had been until recently virtually the whole strength of Birchester's Special Branch, as if he was living in late nineteenth-century London at the time a special branch had been formed at Scotland Yard to combat the Irish dynamiters. Now, with the whole country under the highest level of alert short of imminent attack, he must have as many detectives on call under him as he could ever have dreamt of.

There was little sign of them, however, when, after spending a quarter of an hour briefing ACC Brown, she arrived at Skelton's office, tucked away in the basement of the headquarters building.

She knocked on his door.

'Who is it?'

The question, she thought, was typical of the man who, after a grudging pause, had allowed it to escape his lips. No *Come in* or even a brusquer *Enter*. Just this suspicious demand.

Well, presumably suspicion is his business. Even more, and more permanently, than it's mine.

'Detective Superintendent Martens, wanting a quick word.'

And then she got her 'Oh, come in, come in.'

Skelton, dark-faced – does he shave only every other day, so as to keep that black look? – was sitting at his desk, its surface heaped with dossiers and piled paper. Behind him stood a long row of filing cabinets, reminding her, with a jab of urgency, of the single vandalised cabinet behind Dr Lennox's desk.

'So, Superintendent, what can I do for you? It's a busy time for me, you know.'

Then, as perhaps the fact of her double loss came into his ever-preoccupied mind, he managed to mutter a 'Sorry to hear about...' and look down at the papers in front of him.

'A busy time for all of us,' Harriet said, to hoist him over his embarrassment. 'Do you think a day will come when there's nothing ominous coming our way?'

Skelton glanced up and gave her a *what's this* look.

'The ominous has been with me from the first day I was appointed to this job,' he said. 'And I've no doubt it'll be with me when I hand over to some other poor idiot. You can't have any conception, Mrs Martens, of the mass of possibly dangerous people whose dossiers come into me every day of the week.'

'It's one of those that I've come to ask you about,' Harriet nipped in before more black thoughts could spill out over her. 'A man called Wichmann, Professor Ernst Wichmann.'

Inspector Skelton pushed himself to his feet, turned and nosed his way along the rank of his green filing-cabinets. At last he reached the one that would have been labelled 'W', had his sense of security not left each cabinet unmarked.

He opened one of its two middle drawers, flipped through the files there.

Is each of those without any identification sticker? Harriet mischievously allowed herself to wonder.

But, no. In a moment Skelton pulled out a file, a noticeably thin one, darkened with age. He opened it, peered in.

'Well, he is here,' he said.

'And?'

'Arrived from Germany in 1939. Noted then as a possible infiltrator, a sleeper perhaps.'

'Yes?'

'That's all.'

Harriet could not hold back her astonishment.

'You mean, he, that seventeen-year-old boy, a refugee from the Nazis, has been kept on file as a suspicious individual ever since 1939?'

'It's my duty to keep that file until I receive information that the person named is freed from suspicion, or dead.'

She managed a smile.

'Well, I don't think you'll have Wichmann's file cumbering up your records for very many years more,' she said. 'He's in his eighties. Fit though he looks.'

Her attempt at a lightening humour fell totally flat.

'Nothing more I can help you with then?'

'No. No, nothing, thank you.'

Harriet's visit to Christopher Alexander at home, which she had expected to have to wait till evening to make, came about much earlier. She had rung him at Heronsgate House to fix a time. But the switchboard operator there told her that 'Mr Alexander is no longer with us.'

'No longer with you? Why is that? Is he on leave, or what?'

'I have been told to say no more than I've said to you, madam.'

Harriet thought for a second. Then she went into action.

'I never gave you my name,' she barked. 'But let me tell you now, I am Detective Superintendent Martens, Greater Birchester Police. And I need to interview Mr Alexander. So, tell me, why is it he's *no longer with you?*'

'I— Well, I don't know… The Director—'

'Never mind the Director. Tell me at once why Mr Alexander has left.'

'Well, I suppose you'll find out in some way or another.'

'I will. You can be sure of that. And, if it's any comfort, I can say that if I come to my knowledge of what happened through you, I will not reveal it.'

'Oh. OK then. Chris – that's Christopher – was sacked first thing this morning. Told to clear his desk and that. He just said to me, as he went, that he'd, well, *come unstuck with the boss.* That's what he said.'

'I see. Thank you.'

She rang off, and thought.

Christopher Alexander *unstuck* from Dr Lennox. Why should that be? Has Lennox possibly some grounds for suspicion that Christopher passed on the secret of the hiding-place of the CA 534 to the people who then broke open his secure filing-cabinet? Or can Christopher, conscience-stricken, have simply confessed he had passed on what he knew? What if all he did was mention to someone that Lennox was defying the order to destroy the specimen of CA 534 – But to whom? Whom? – and then had felt he ought to own up? Yes, this perhaps was more likely for the high-minded young man who had felt he was unfit to tackle writing a DLitt on— Damn it, on... No. Yes, got it. On Jean Paul Richter, a barely known German writer who was held in high esteem by Professor Wichmann and is mentioned in a Sherlock Holmes story.

No doubt about it. I must go to Christopher's flat at once – good thing I noted his name and address – and make sure, if he *is* somehow a link to some terrorist organisation, that he's not on the point of going into hiding or even trying to get out of the country.

Harriet had some difficulty finding space to park outside the house where Christopher Alexander had told her he lived. The street was evidently heavily occupied by young people working in the centre of the city, and their cars, a motley collection of far from gleaming vehicles, were ranged along both sides of it, almost nose to tail, looking miserably depressing in the chilly rain that had begun to fall. One of them, directly outside the house whose number Christopher had given her, was particularly irritating. An ancient Mini, much battered but painted in compensation in badly applied psychedelic colours, had been parked wildly askew, carelessly occupying most of two possible spaces.

But Harriet stopped herself cursing its owner, or even getting on to the local police station to suggest someone come round and take its number. She had a task ahead.

She drove quickly to a neighbouring street where she

managed to find somewhere to put the car – even without a
yellow line – then marched back through the rain up to the
door of the house, found which of the eight bell-pushes she
ought to ring, and pressed hard on it.

As, at last, she heard steps coming to the door, she ran
through in her mind the various possibilities she might
encounter. A warily defensive young man preparing to go
into hiding, or just a shocked and perhaps tearful young
man unexpectedly fired from his job, or even a wildly
terrified young man holding a gun.

What she saw when the door opened was Christopher
Alexander looking in no way different from the person she
had interviewed in his cubbyhole of an office. His almost
feminine roses-and-cream cheeks were just as they had been
when she had first seen him. His big eyes were innocently
blinking. His thatch of fair hair, if not smoothly brushed,
was only a little tousled, as if from time to time he had
worriedly run his hands through it.

'Oh. Oh, it's you,' he said.

'Yes, Detective Superintendent Martens.'

Although she had hoped that by formally stating her
name and rank she would get a reaction from him, nothing
happened.

He simply stood there, still blinking.

Attempting to prevent me entering? Prevent me seeing
preparations for flight? Bewildered to find me here? Or,
with evidence on display connecting him to some terrorist
outfit, determined that I shan't see it?

'I'd like a word inside,' she said, hoping the blunt
approach would make him reveal something of his state of
mind.

For a moment he stood there still. Then he stepped back.

'Yes, yes. Er— Come in. Come up. Yes.'

She followed him to the flat, which seemed to consist of
no more than a cramped living-room and, with its door
wide open, an equally small bedroom filled almost entirely
by a double mattress on the floor, the duvet on it thrown

back.

So, that girl, Maggie what's-her-name, here last night? No doubt, if I was to conduct a full-scale search I'd find the good old *traces d'amour* on that mattress, however little she had matched up as a lover to Tim Patterson's expectations. But stains like that would hardly tell me anything more than I know already. Might make an excuse and have a look at the bathroom though. Often says more about the people who use it than whatever they choose to say out loud.

'Sit down, please,' Christopher said, lifting a stack of newspapers and paperbacks off a small armchair and plonking himself on another at the scarred and scratched light-wood table tucked under the single window.

Glancing at the books, as he piled them straighter beside him, Harriet saw they were mostly science-fiction titles. She took that as a way to begin.

'I see you don't have much intention of going back to your German studies,' she said, gesturing at the pile. 'Who was it Professor Wichmann told me you'd been going to do a DLitt on? Richter, John-something Richter?'

'Jean Paul Richter,' Christopher said.

And shut up.

'But I'm right in thinking,' Harriet ploughed on, 'that you've got the opportunity of going back to the university – now you're no longer at Heronsgate House?'

'But I won't,' he said with more terse confidence than she had expected.

Oh, no, young man, you're not going to cut me off like that. I'm going to put my finger on more about you. A lot more.

'Oh, why is that? Professor Wichmann told me you might well have had a good career as an academic.'

This sideways approach did seem to get more of a reaction.

Christopher's pink and white cheeks were flooded by a cherry-bright blush.

'I—' he said. 'Oh, I don't know. I— Well, I'd be mostly

all on my own doing that. And— And, well, really I like to have someone there, someone sort of directly above me, who'd keep me on the straight path.'

Yes, as I thought, more or less. Total lack of self-confidence. Which tells me what? Almost anything, I guess. Still, keep it in mind.

'But how did your leaving Heronsgate House come about?' she asked, hoping to find a less buttoned-up answer now that he had admitted to some of his troubles. 'When I saw you there, you seemed to be well entrenched.'

'Yes.'

That and no more.

She cursed.

Oyster, oyster, I'm going to prize open that surprisingly tough shell of yours, whether you like it or not.

'So what happened?' she persisted sharply. 'How, within the space of a few hours, did you go from holding down the job of PA to the Director to being totally unemployed?'

'I just did.'

'Come on, I need to know. You can hardly have forgotten that on Tuesday night a number of men forced their way into Heronsgate House, broke open the secure cabinet in the Director's office and stole a highly dangerous herbicide.'

'I haven't forgotten.'

'So?'

'What more is there to say about it?'

'A good deal, I should think, since it seems to have brought about your sudden dismissal. If that's what took place. Did it?'

'Yes.'

'Come on now, Christopher, I need to know exactly what happened. You must see that it may be relevant to my inquiries.'

For a moment he sat there at the table, the awkwardly-piled books beside him, and said nothing. Then he gave her his answer.

'Dr Lennox blamed me for it.'

'For the break-in? Why? Why should he blame you? You led me to understand that all you did was to find that drawer forced, usher out the cleaning lady and phone Dr Lennox. Did you do more than that? Did you have some other security duties, ones that Dr Lennox had given you confidentially? And ones you failed to carry out?'

'No, no. He didn't do anything like that. I— I think what had made him angry was his suspicion that I would leak things he didn't want to come out. I mean, he knew that I knew that fellow Tim Patterson of the *Star*. I'd told him so, when Tim got hold of that story about the existence of the CA 491, though I swore I hadn't passed it on.'

'But had you?'

'No. No, really I hadn't. It was only…'

'Yes?'

'Well, I think Tim could have got the first hint of it from me when I— I was sort of boasting one evening about the importance of the work we did at Heronsgate House. But I didn't give him any details. Not one. But what I'd said may have put him on to the chap who did tell Tim about it. You remember I told you about all that.'

'Yes, you did, though you wouldn't give me the fellow's name. However, I know it now. Oliphant.'

'Oh. Oh, but… Well, I suppose it can't be helped. He's in Australia now.'

'Yes, I know that, too. But what I don't know is why Dr Lennox pushed you out, without a moment's notice. You had, as they say, to clear your desk and leave.'

'Yes.'

'Come on, I need to know more. Did Dr Lennox tell you explicitly why he was sacking you, what he thought you'd done?'

'Well, yes. But…'

'But what?'

'I'm not meant to say.'

'But you're going to. I'm a police officer, let me remind

you. I have powers of arrest.'

'No. No, you mustn't.'

Harriet noted, not without a certain grim pleasure, that Christopher now was looking thoroughly scared.

'I'm considering it,' she said.

'Well, yes, then. I will tell you. I've got to. Yes, it's this. Dr Lennox made me sign an undertaking. A solemn undertaking that I would never say anything about the circumstances of the theft that night. You won't let him know I have, will you?'

You poor innocent young man. Really, you'd be much better safely tucked up in the world of academia.

'You can trust me,' she said to him. 'Unless it becomes a matter for the courts. But what is it, do you think, that Dr Lennox doesn't want you to reveal in any circumstances?'

Have I got – never mind by what roundabout way – to some key point?

Christopher sat there. She could see his Adam's apple moving up and down in his throat.

One more prompt?

No. Here it comes.

'I don't know. I don't really know. Unless...'

'Unless?'

Christopher shifted about on his chair. His elbow brushed the heaped books at his side. A few cascaded to the floor.

When he straightened up from gathering them together he looked more in charge of himself.

'It's like this,' he said. 'It may be that Dr Lennox, though he didn't specifically say it to me, thought that there was something... Well, something odd about the way that the top drawer of his cabinet had been pushed out of shape. I mean, I suppose it was done with... With some sort of – what do you call it? – some sort of jemmy. Crowbar. But— But, well, the drawer didn't seem damaged enough to have been forced in that way. Or I didn't think so. And Dr Lennox may have thought the same.'

'And didn't want you to go telling the world, telling me, about that?'

'Well, yes.'

'I hardly think something like that would make Dr Lennox insist on you signing that undertaking. Did he give you any other reason for asking for it?'

'Well, no. No, he just said I had to sign it. He said it was the customary thing when confidential work is involved.'

'All right. We'll leave it at that.'

Christopher at once looked relieved.

'But,' she said sharply, 'if any other thoughts occur to you, get in touch with me. About anything, no matter how trivial it might seem. Here's my mobile number again.'

'Yes, yes. I will. Of course, I will. Thank you.'

But Harriet hadn't quite finished.

'One thing,' she said, 'do you mind if I use your loo before I go?'

Christopher, naïve Christopher, seemed almost as much put out by this request from a woman – a lady – as he had been by the probing questions she had asked.

'Oh. The loo? Yes. Yes, please do. I mean, it— It's the only other door on the landing. It's in the bathroom.'

Harriet did not wait for embarrassed Christopher to say more.

She got to her feet, picked up her handbag by its shoulder strap. Marched out.

In the bathroom she shut and bolted the door and then gave the little white-tiled room a methodical survey.

Yes, plenty of useful insights on the two people who use it. Two tubes of toothpaste on the rather spattered glass shelf above the wash-basin, different brands. His, probably the big Aquafresh, hers the smaller one, half-used, extra-whitening Arm and Hammer. Hadn't Tim Patterson talked about her 'white-teeth smile'? So, Maggie – yes – Quirke co-habiting here, even without evidence of *traces d'amour*. And I wouldn't be altogether surprised if she isn't the first woman naïve Christopher has slept with. I can see the narrow single bed he had being replaced – how exciting for him – by the mattress on the floor. And, yes, all this would account for those unexpected bouts of confidence just now. A first girlfriend. A young man's triumphing. Young love. Those sweet, liberating exchanges of secrets. Unburdening.

Then something she had taken in without realising it as she surveyed the little room brought all her sentimental thoughts tumbling to the ground. The mess that Christopher, Christopher undoubtedly, had left everywhere. The top of his toothpaste not put back, a dark line of urine drops across the worn pink mat round the toilet bowl, the door of the little medicine cupboard left ajar – quick peek inside, heap of multi-buy orange razors, usual contraceptive pills – and even a discarded pair of bright-coloured shorts kicked into a corner to be picked up later. Boys' untidiness. The sort of untidiness Graham and Malcolm had always left in the bathroom at home before they had gone off, carefree, to college.

God, she thought then in a sudden blast of black remembrance, Graham, Malcolm. I must get out of here. I must. I must.

She caught hold of the door-bolt, wrenched it clear, pulled the door open.

And then... Then Hologram Harriet made her appearance once more. She turned back, flushed the loo as if she had used it.

But Real Harriet, not even calling out good-bye to Christopher, pulled the house door wide open, rushed out and stood there in the rain letting black thoughts race and tumble through her head. Graham dead. Dead when he had promised so much. Malcolm, there in St Mary's, perhaps crippled for life.

Chapter Eight

When Harriet had recovered herself enough, just enough, to ring John at his office she learnt that he had, as usual, been in touch with St Mary's and had had yet better news of Malcolm.

'They say his condition's stable and he's going to be transferred to an ordinary ward. Some time this afternoon. We shall be able to visit him this evening, they're giving us special treatment. They suggested between seven and eight, if that suits you.'

'Yes, yes, that'll be fine. I'll see that it is. Oh, John, this is good, isn't it? I almost begin to... Well, to hope for his complete recovery.'

'Yes. Yes, I did too, for a bit. But, darling, don't let yourself think it's happened already, or even that it will finally. There's a long way to go yet. And... And, Harriet, there's another thing.'

'Yes?'

'I've arranged the funeral. I fixed it for this day fortnight. The hospital is happy to leave Graham where he is till then. They've been very good about everything. But I had a call from that Superintendent Robertson at Notting Hill, and he's very keen that there should be a full-scale funeral, as an opportunity for the Met to show solidarity. I gather the Commissioner himself wants to be present. So I didn't think we could do anything else but go for that, though for myself...'

'For me, too,' Harriet said. 'A quiet cremation. But, yes, I can see, when they're wanting to do all that, then we must let them. So this day fortnight. Right.'

God, she thought, John's good to me. He knew, he must have done, how I couldn't cope with the thought that there had to be a formal funeral for Graham, the standing at the graveside, or watching the coffin slide away, and he just took it all into his own hands. And now it's arranged, and I can bear to know that it's going to happen. I can cope.

And at once, in the way that the mind works, the very opposite thought about John came into her head.

Last night, up at St Mary's when he so suddenly rounded on me. Said all those unbearable things, made those accusations, that I had somehow forced and bullied the twins into joining the Service, that it was because I wanted successors to myself in the police. All right, he calmed down soon enough. He even told me, because he saw how much he'd wounded me, deeply hurt me, that he hadn't meant what he said.

But had he after all? Isn't it possible that for these last couple of years, ever since the question of what the twins were going to do came up, he's been nursing a grudge against me? Because, it seemed to him, by cajoling them into joining the Met I was thoughtlessly risking their lives when I knew what the security situation was and threatened to continue to be. And more, can there have been other things he's been holding against me? Perhaps for years, perhaps from as soon as the first few wildly happy months of our wedded life had gone by? What things I don't know, but there could have been things. Held against me day after day, year after year, and nothing ever said.

And then, when, like me, he was acutely afraid for Malcolm, that he might at any moment slip away to join Graham in death, everything that had festered there for so long erupted out. Not *in vino veritas* but *in* – what's the word? – *in timor veritas.*

She stood where she was, in the street just a few yards from Christopher Alexander's flat, her mobile still clutched in her hand, and surrendered to the welter of storm-dark clouds tossing and racing through her head.

She fought, at last, for calm.

Christ, I'm a police officer, a detective. I'm tasked with investigating the break-in at Heronsgate House, something threatening perhaps the whole of the British Isles, the whole countryside, bringing – it could be – ruin and

starvation to us all. And what am I doing? I'm letting my
own emotions, my own personal troubles, swamp every
action I should be taking.

And, standing here indulging myself in these hysterical
thoughts I'm even forgetting what I should be doing for
Malcolm. For Malcolm, not now in intensive care but in an
ordinary hospital bed, able to speak more than a few broken
phrases, and needing now, more than ever, the support of
his parents. My support, John's support.

She realised she was still holding the mobile, tapped out
John's number again.

'John?'

'Harriet? You again. Is everything all right?'

'Yes, yes. Why— Why did you ask?'

'Well, you sounded rather, I don't know, strained.'

'But I only just said your name.'

'I know. But... Well, are you all right?'

'Yes,' she answered. 'Yes, I am. Now. But you spotted it.
I wasn't, till just a moment ago, feeling all right. I was
having some sort of a brainstorm or something, got at by all
kinds of nightmare thoughts. But clever of you, more than
clever, to have heard all that in one single word of mine.'

'Long years of marriage,' John replied.

But, however much that was touched by a certain
dryness, it brought to Harriet a surge of reassurance.

No, someone who understands me so well, right to that
extent, cannot have been harbouring and harbouring those
vicious thoughts I believed were deep in his mind. I've been
a fool. Even if – Graham and Malcolm – I was perhaps
entitled to be.

'John,' she said quietly into the mobile, 'I never asked,
just now, but do we have to wait till tonight to see
Malcolm? Can it be this afternoon? John, I think we should
go as soon as we possibly can.'

'So we should. Where are you now?'

She had to think for a moment.

'I'm somewhere not far from the University area,' she

said at last. 'Outside a flat where I've been questioning someone.'

'All right. You've got your car, I suppose?'

Have I? Oh, of course I have. It's there. Just round the corner.

'Yes, I came here in it.'

'Right then, go home, and I'll meet you there. When we've had a bite of lunch we'll head off down the motorway.'

Arriving home, however, something altogether unexpected awaited her. When she began to open the door she found it obstructed. Stooping down, after a harder push had done nothing to clear the obstruction, she put an arm through the narrow gap she had created and felt about.

Letters. Dozens of them.

And then she realised. They must be letters of condolence delivered during the morning.

And I simply never thought they would be bound to come. So many reminders of what I half-wanted to be able to forget.

She stood up then feeling – she knew she ought not to – a dull growing rage, rage against all these well-meaning people, all their friends, their good friends, who were intruding on her, forcing her to think of Graham, to admit to her mind the full weight of that great blank, black loss.

She drew in a long breath.

No. No, I mustn't. They may help. What's been written inside all those white, blue, grey envelopes may help.

Gritting her teeth hard together, as she found she had to, she stooped again and managed to brush the pile clear.

But, with the door properly open, she could do no more at first then stare down at the tossed-about heap.

Then, at last, she reached forward, picked out the first letter that her fingers came in contact with, took it up, peered at the handwriting of the address – didn't recognise it, blockish somehow – and ripped it open.

There was only one word written in the same crude hand

on the single sheet of white paper she had pulled out.

Traitor.

For what seemed like long minutes she stood there, her eyes fixed on the seven black-ink letters. And then, trickling into her brain, came the knowledge of why they had been scrawled there.

That TV interview. What I said at the end of it. What was forced out of me. What I found I believed. And to this person what I said must have seemed like an insult, an insult to the fighters in the War on Terror to which they had given their belief.

She let the sheet flutter to the floor. Then with her foot pushed away the rest of the pile – it can't all be as horrible as that – and staggering into the sitting-room, dropped, a deadweight, into a chair.

It was there that John, arriving only ten or fifteen minutes later, found her.

For the third time in as many days, Harriet realised, with a sense of shock at the suddenness with which her life had been transformed, she was sitting beside John heading along the motorway through steady rain towards London and St Mary's Hospital. Good God, she thought, was it only on Tuesday that we were talking about distant thunder and the meaning it somehow carried with it and then the phone rang and heavy-voiced Superintendent Robertson told me about Graham and Malcolm?

She took a look at John.

Yes, as I might have expected, zipping us along, as calmly and confidently as when he had told me that I mustn't let that letter, that word *Traitor*, get to me.

'Darling,' he'd said, 'you have to remember the person who wrote that, man or woman, may well have lost a son in the sort of war that's being fought, just as we have. They're in as precarious a state as you are, as I am. Just let it pass till we both feel more able to cope. We won't even open any of the other letters. I'll put them away in the spare room cupboard till we feel strong enough. What we've got to do now is to see Malcolm, encourage him, reassure ourselves.'

'I was just thinking,' she said now, 'it was just a week ago – no, less, less – that we were having that discussion about how oddly threatening even a single far-off peal of thunder can seem, when the phone rang and—'

She balked at the words she had been about to say, despite having already uttered them in her mind.

'And we heard,' John supplied.

'Yes, we heard about that devilish bomb.'

Then into her head there came another totally unconnected recollection.

'John, there's something I've been meaning to ask you. It's absurd. I'd forgotten all about it. But now suddenly, thinking about that awful moment, it's somehow come back. It's this. In the course, as we say, of my inquiries I was talking to that dreadful reporter on the *Star*, Tim Patterson. I asked him how he'd come to know what research they were doing at Heronsgate House, and he patted himself on the back about another scoop he'd had, something to do with some funny little organisation called… Can't quite remember. Some ridiculous name. But, whatever it was, he said that a relation of yours was a member of it. He boasted his story had resulted in a bunch of them coming up before the magistrates. I don't know which of your—'

'But I do,' John broke in. 'It'd be Aunty Beryl. Not in fact an aunt at all, but an elderly distant-ish cousin. She was actually at our wedding, but I doubt if you've seen her since. I do sometimes go and visit her when you're working on a Sunday for some reason. I've never liked to ask you to come with me. She's a bit difficult, never married and poor as your church mouse. Left a little bit when her mother died, but in such a way it's paid out the same amount for all the years since, while good old inflation's gone up and up.'

He made a face.

'Oh, dear. I haven't been round for weeks and weeks now. Somehow let the time slip by. I ought to have done, though. She lives a pretty miserable life, shut up most of the time in an awful tiny flat. In Moorfields of all miserable places, all she can afford. There she is, absolutely afraid to go out at night because she thinks she'll be mugged, and living mostly, I suspect, on tea, bread-and-butter and baked beans.'

'Well, I certainly don't remember ever having met her, even at the wedding. All I can remember about that is my old Uncle Michael, all dressed up in morning coat and whatnot after years and years, and never realising his top hat still had dried lavender leaves in it. They were stuck with sweat all over his forehead.'

'Oh, yes, I remember him, though, like you, the rest of that day's just a blur for me.'

'I'm glad you're as bad as I am. But, yes, your Aunty Beryl's very likely the one Tim Patterson mentioned to me. He said she'd been up in court because she was involved in something called Waggy. Not a name, initials. WAGI, Women Against something or other.'

'Genetic Interference.'

'Oh, John, how is it you always know everything?'

'In this instance simply because Aunty Beryl does belong to that ridiculous outfit, and I had to stump up to pay her fine for her share in cutting down a field of GM maize.'

'Simple explan— Oh, wait. John, can it be that Waggy would be interested in the runaway herbicide, CA 534?'

'Oh, I very much doubt it. WAGI's an absolutely tinpot affair, and an all-women one too. They made a real mess-up of their attack on that maize field. So I can't see them actually breaking in anywhere, let alone at dead of night.'

'No. No, neither can I. Especially as the intruders – keep this under your hat – appear to have been a pretty nasty bunch of professionals.'

'Oh, were they? Well, that lets Aunty Beryl off any list of suspects you may have. I'd even say the Number One at WAGI, a much more frighteningly ferocious old lady called, I think, Tritton, Miss Gwendoline Tritton, is not worth adding to that list.'

'No, I shouldn't think she would be. I suppose it's possible, though, that she might have managed to employ the toughs who poured petrol over one of the security guards. But I can't see someone like her even knowing how to get hold of them.'

She lapsed into silence then as the motorway came to an end and John sat a little further forward in his seat, negotiating the London traffic coming jockeying in on his right.

So, finding their way to Malcolm's ward at St Mary's, all thoughts of theft of the CA 534 and the potential disaster it threatened, even set against the appalling EuroVin havoc, went out of Harriet's head.

Malcolm? How are we going to find him? Better than when we last saw him? Or deteriorated in some way? Even back in intensive care?

In a moment her questions were answered. Malcolm, though flat on his back and with a blanket tent over his legs, was immediately responsive as they came into his sight.

'Mum, Dad, good to see you.'

A wide smile.

Which, at once, was replaced by an acute grimace of pain. His face went in an instant white as bone.

'Malcolm, what is it?' Harriet shot out. 'Shall we call a nurse? Or— Or—'

'No, it's OK really. It's just— Just that sometimes I get dead scared of— Of what may happen, you know.'

God, what can I say, Harriet asked herself. It's true, after all. He is in danger of death still. I can't bear it.

But John was coming to the rescue.

'Understandable, Malcolm, old fellow,' he said. 'I'd be scared in your situation. Anybody would. But, from what the medics tell us, you haven't really all that much to fear now.'

Malcolm managed a smile, if a pallid one.

'It's just that every now and again a spasm of something down below sets me off,' he said. 'Can't tell which leg it comes from, actually. They're both quite a mess. But it passes away. Gone now, in fact.'

So they sat on, exchanging news. He told them about the treatment he was having. 'I'm under a Sir. See that board above the bed. His name there in beautifully painted letters.'

They both contrived to respond with a laugh. More of which, encouragingly, came and went as they told him that life in Birchester was going on much as usual, despite all the police activity and the papers and TV still being full of the EuroVin bloodbath.

Then, to her surprise, Malcolm abruptly put a sharp question.

'Look, there's something I want to know. Those people who planted the booby trap that caught us, some Indians I heard on the TV news. What were they aiming to achieve?'

Harriet was immediately baffled. But John, she found, was not.

'Yes, I can tell you something about them,' he said. 'I've been making some inquiries. They belong, it seems, to something called – can't remember exactly – Hindu Marg or something, means more or less India's Way. It's a protest organisation dedicated to ending what they see as wicked Western influences. They're anti-American, of course, very down apparently on Hollywood films, which are extremely popular there. But also, in view of what you might sum up as "the days of the Raj", they're strongly anti-British. Cricket, also of course immensely popular in India, gets a pasting from them. Naturally, too, and perhaps rather more understandably, all missionaries are wickedest of the wicked. Big international firms come in for stick as well. And, when I say they're *dedicated*, I mean they're violent. Apparently the most recent British affront to them was a comedy film made here, not very successful, but now being shown in India, called, yes, *Here Come the Kapoors*. Arson attacks because of that.'

Harriet was horrified.

'And because of— Of this comedy film,' she burst out, 'they planted that booby- trap bomb that killed Graham. Killed him. Just because of that.'

'Yes,' John replied. 'Though I'm surprised that— Well, that you're surprised. You should know, more than most people with the work you're doing, that terrorism is, if you like, the new revolutionary idea. I think it probably springs from the effect of the destruction of the Twin Towers. Nasty eyes lit up then all over the world.'

'And is anybody doing anything about it?' came Malcolm's voice from the bed. 'Is anybody doing anything about their threat, saw it on the TV there, to go on planting bombs here until we yield to their impossible demands?'

'Well, it's the usual thing,' John answered. 'What's always said when there's anything like this. *We cannot yield to terrorism, or we will be under threat for ever more.*' A bite of a laugh.

'So what's happened since 9/11? We're all of us under more threats than ever, that's what. All sorts of people have seen how, if you're prepared to risk your life for any cause, you've got an extraordinarily powerful weapon in your hands. But, look at it the other way round, there's the perfectly good argument that, if we do yield, it will still, in fact, encourage all these mad groups to go further and do worse.'

'So here I am with my legs under this tent thing,' Malcolm said, with remarkable cheerfulness.

He let his eyes stray to the TV screen high on the wall opposite. *EastEnders* had just begun. A fight was brewing.

'And here I'll stay,' he added, still smiling, 'till my legs get strong enough for me to totter out.'

In the car on the way back – the rain had not stopped – those happily optimistic parting words came back to Harriet with a whole extra meaning.

They'd been driving for less than half an hour, just entering the motorway, when John put in a careful question:

'Listen, what do you actually feel about those people, the India's Way lot?'

'Oh, I know why you're asking,' she said. 'You were surprised when you'd produced your potted history that I didn't leap up, all guns firing, and swear I was going to see the criminals who set that booby trap go to prison for the rest of their lives.'

'Well, I was surprised for a moment. I hadn't actually intended to say anything about them to Malcolm, at least not until I'd seen he was on firmer ground. But when he put that sudden question, I felt I had to be as frank in answering.'

He turned his head and gave her a quick smile.

'It was for much the same reasons that I've been holding back from telling you what I'd found out about that lot. I didn't know whether you'd be ready to take it. Equally, at St Mary's just now, I thought you must be managing to restrain yourself because you didn't want to excite Malcolm.'

'Yes, that was what did make me keep my big mouth shut, at least while we were still sitting with him.'

She spent a moment getting her thoughts in order.

'But,' she said eventually, 'it was the way Malcolm looked at it all, what he said just before we went, that stopped me exploding as soon as we were out of the ward there. I was all ready to, I promise you. Boiling over in fact. But then I saw in my mind's eye, Malcolm lying there as we'd seen him, with God knows what had been done to his legs under that tent thing. And I thought that shouting and cursing, which was what I was about to do, would get me nowhere. If Malcolm, never the soul of patience as we well know, could take it as philosophically as that, then who was I not to try to put it all into place myself?'

'I'm not the one to say you were wrong,' John replied, easing his foot a little from the gas pedal. 'You often enough get irritated with me for not reacting to things in your fiery manner, so when for once you take the long view then I can only say *Well done.*'

'Thank you, kind sir.'

She fell silent, thoughts unravelling themselves little by little.

Yes, Malcolm's cheerful acceptance of what had happened to him, of Graham's death too, is one spark of brightness. One spark in a world seemingly darker and darker under clouds of doubt and dismay. Look at me. If the people who put Malcolm where he is are still there, untouched, what about the people supposedly in my own sights? At any time now they, too, are likely to make demands, backed up by the threat of using that CA 534 to cut huge destructive swathes through all the countryside. And what am I doing, what can I really do, to stop them?

Into her mind then there popped, incongruously, a fragment of a schooldays camp-fire chant.

> *One man went to mow*
> *Went to mow a meadow.*
> *One man and his dog*
> *Went to mow a meadow.*

Oh, yes, she thought. But it's not with a dog that the man's gone to mow. It's with that small box of ultra destructive CA 534. Or... Or, if it's a different man, a different man with a different cause, it could be just *one man and his bomb.*

Chapter Nine

In the morning, lying in bed for a last few snatched minutes, Harriet found herself full of doubts about the next move in her investigation. She stopped the wild sweep of thoughts racing through her head, and began again. Now she found there was something. It might be the merest wisp of a hope, but it was there.

Didn't I learn only yesterday afternoon something about an organisation as absurd and perhaps as ambitious as India's Way? All right, a good deal more absurd. But, if what John's just been saying has any substance to it, then even as ridiculous an organisation as— As waggy old WAGI could somehow be behind that break-in. They could have just as many impossible ambitions as India's Way. So could this be, just possibly, the tiny glim of fire that lights a fuse running to where the gunpowder barrel's hidden?

So, yes. Yes, I'm going to get hold of, not John's Aunty Beryl, but WAGI's Number One. What did John call her? Yes, I'm going to have a word, perhaps a very useful word, with frighteningly ferocious Miss Gwendoline Tritton. John went on to say to me, sitting in the car going up to London, that Gwendoline Tritton was hardly worth thinking about. That she was no more than some sort of elderly madwoman, and the organisation she heads was, John's word, *tinpot*?

All right, John made light of her. Wasn't his *frighteningly ferocious* a distinct put-down? Even a typical male put-down? And, sensible though John is, aren't there times when the not-sensible approach pays off? The leap in the dark? Hasn't it done so more than once in my time as a detective?

OK, there may be better lines to explore. Professor Wichmann, nice old boy though he seemed, told me nothing that clearly put him out of account, and pretty Christopher Alexander, since his instant dismissal from

Heronsgate House has become, really, more likely to be the person who, perhaps unwittingly, tipped off those men who fought and bullied their way to that insecure security cabinet.

But, wait. Wait. What about Christopher's newly-acquired girlfriend, Maggie, the white-smiling marathon runner? Didn't Tim say she had been a member of WAGI? If so, Gwendoline Tritton could possibly have learnt through Maggie something she'd found out, in some way or another, from her new boyfriend. It could have been where Dr Lennox had locked away the CA 534. If so, Gwendoline Tritton might well have seen its potential as a weapon to enable tinpot WAGI to threaten even the Government.

She threw back the duvet.

Out of the house before the post had come, with its dreaded new batch of not-to-be-read condolence letters, dismissing all thoughts of that ominous single word *Traitor*, Harriet, by the time she reached her office at HQ, had decided on as cautious an approach to Gwendoline Tritton as John himself might have used in some intricate negotiation at mighty Majestic Insurance. From Birchester's electoral roll she found where Miss Tritton lived, but set off first for her nearest police station. After all, hadn't the lady been fined for her part in burning that field of GM maize? So she must be, in the old phrase, known to the police.

And known she was.

'Gwendoline Tritton,' DI Weston, in charge of the CID there, said, eyes lifted to heaven. '*That* woman.'

He listed then, for Harriet's benefit, a whole catalogue of crimes. None had been so serious as to lead any of the magistrates she had appeared before to impose a prison sentence. But time and again she had been fined, for public order offences, for obstruction, for breaches of the Queen's Peace. Once she had even been charged with being in possession of a firearm without a licence, though that had turned out to be no more than a replica handgun acquired for protection against burglars. Nor were her activities on behalf of Women Against Genetic Interference the only reason for her defiance of civil authority. Over the years, it appeared, she had belonged to various organisations devoted to every sort of protest, very often at the head of them.

'All those fines were no skin off her nose,' DI Weston added. 'She's one rich lady. Sole remaining heir from the pre-plastic days when Birchester firms supplied half the world with leather goods.'

'That's interesting.'

'Bear it in mind if you're going to interview her. It makes her a bloody awkward cuss.'

Or, Harriet registered, in John's rather more literary terms, *frighteningly ferocious*.

Arriving, by appointment, at The Willows in Pargeter Avenue, one of the few remaining respectable streets in the run-down Meads area, Harriet found at the door, not a maid in uniform, but Miss Gwendoline Tritton herself, the sole inhabitant, it appeared, of the whole big house. Awkwardly tall, in her late seventies, very probably a full eighty, she stood squarely at the large heavily carved front door, feet in stout, faded blue trainers rooted to the mat. A long, rough woollen skirt in a pattern of large orange and yellow squares hid much of her legs, but what could be seen of them were stockingless, sturdy as little tree-trunks, and as gnarled. Above the skirt came a jacket of dull green wool, fastened all the way up to the neck by small knobby, leather-covered buttons. And, above the jacket, her deeply wrinkled face, partly masked by a pair of heavy-rimmed spectacles, was dominated by a considerable pointed nose.

Before she had said even a word, Harriet was visited by an image of a brown female blackbird vigorously attacking the earth of an autumn flowerbed, aggressive beak flicking away to left and right every concealing red or brown leaf.

'Detective Superintendent Martens, I suppose,' she said at last, her high-pitched voice penetrating most likely all the way to the far side of the wide road beyond.

'Yes. It's good of you to see me at such short notice.'

'You had better come in. I've no intention of discussing my affairs out in public.'

Harriet followed her then into a large ground-floor drawing-room. Although office, she thought, might be a better description. True, at the far end there were three or four armchairs round the empty fireplace, with between them small tables on which in more distant days delicate teacups might have rested. But otherwise the room was occupied by a long, bare-wood trestle table, covered from end to end with piles of leaflets in different bright, attention-seeking colours, boxes of stationery, piles of newspaper cuttings held down by a variety of unorthodox paperweights, and a whole heap of saved copies of the *Birchester Chronicle*. Nearby stood a computer work-station, printer ready beside it.

And up against the walls were two rows of tall, old wooden filing-cabinets. With all the swiftness of a bungee jumper's elastic cord, they sent Harriet's thoughts back to the dented top drawer of Dr Lennox's smart silvery-grey security cabinet.

As soon as they had entered, Gwendoline Tritton had swung round to prevent Harriet going further in.

'So,' she said, 'to what do I owe the honour of a visit from a senior officer of the Greater Birchester Police? Not, I imagine, to a request for a contribution to your Benevolent Fund, that convenient fiction for the more overt sort of bribe.'

'No,' Harriet replied, registering that hostilities had clearly commenced, 'this is more of a personal matter.'

'Personal, I suppose, to me.'

Two long bony fingers tapped emphatically on the top button of the green jacket.

'Yes, to you,' Harriet conceded.

'Then, let me say, I consider it outrageous that you should come here making inquiries about my personal circumstances. We have enough of a police state already in this country without officers badgering citizens in their own homes.'

'Well, we do try to avoid that. But I confess I'm wondering to what extent this is your own home. Certainly, the room here has all the appearance of a business office.'

'And what if it does? Cannot any private citizen conduct a business in her own house, if she's so willing? I use this room as the headquarters of the organisation, Women Against Genetic Interference. I should suppose you, as a woman, would have more sympathy for such a cause than your average authoritarian police officer. You yourself, don't forget, are a victim at every moment of the day of genetic interference of one sort or another.'

'That is as may be,' Harriet answered, 'however, I am here, not as a woman, but as one of the authoritarian officers you seem to hold in such low esteem. And, as such, I have some questions I need to ask about your organisation.'

'Then I must tell you that I refuse to answer.' Tap, tap again from long fingers in the region of the breastbone. 'Your presence here is utterly uncalled for. The sooner you leave the better.'

'No. I am a police officer entitled to question any person whose activities may be of an illegal nature.'

For a tense moment Harriet and Gwendoline Tritton faced each other, each unwaveringly staring.

But it was Gwendoline Tritton who broke.

'Very well,' she said, as if merely exasperated. 'I suppose, as you're here, I may as well answer whatever impertinent questions you may want to put to me.'

'Oh, they're none of them very impertinent. It's simply that I am currently the officer in the Greater Birchester force charged with making a survey of the security risks to the city in the wake of the Hasselburg tragedy. It has been brought to my attention that WAGI, although it is not, of course, a major terrorist organisation, has in recent years used on occasion violent methods to publicise its aims. There has not always been enough evidence for proceedings to be taken, but we have had some reason to believe that the intimidating phone messages which some genetics scientists have received may have come from members of your organisation.'

Slow up, slow up. This damned woman has somehow caused me to say too much. Is all this about intimidating phone messages going too far?

Well, I'm committed to it, so carry on. Drawing in my horns, if I can.

'Consequently, Miss Tritton, I need to know whether WAGI intends to continue these and similar activities. If so, they are likely, I scarcely need to point out to you, to hinder efforts to protect the citizens of Birchester from the slaughter brought about at Hasselburg.'

Gwendoline Tritton tossed her head.

'Just as I thought,' she said, 'a police scheme to stop WAGI carrying out its wholly worthwhile aims by pretending other issues are involved. Absolutely outrageous.'

'I think not. Let me give you an instance of what might happen. As you must know, we in the West are now threatened by al-Qaeda and its offshoot organisations targeting any large gathering like the EuroVin festival with the sole purpose of killing as great a number of innocent people as possible.'

'More nonsense. We in the West, forsooth.'

Forsooth, Harriet thought. She really did say *forsooth*. What a dinosaur of a woman.

'All that,' Gwendoline Tritton steam-rollered on, 'is nothing but politicians contriving that whatever it suits them to encourage, such as the manufacture of genetically harmful foods purely for profit, shall go on without hindrance. I shall certainly not take one single step to assist you in inquiries of this sort.'

'Nevertheless, I require from you an assurance that

WAGI's current aims do not include the use or the threat of violence. The lives of hundreds, even thousands, of Birchester people may be at risk from your incidental activities.'

'Incidental? Let me tell you WAGI's aims are far from incidental. What we are attempting to do goes to the very heart of present-day society. It is time, it is more than time, that people realised that they are being subjected, women especially, to the most ruthless campaign of misdirection and plain lying there has ever been, just so as to keep the public in ignorance of what truly affects them.'

'I won't attempt to quarrel with that analysis, Miss Tritton, though perhaps I could. But I will ask, once more, whether your organisation's attempts to inform the public of your concerns or, indeed, to change the situation, will involve any degree of violent activity?'

'I cannot divulge our confidential decisions.'

She folded her arms across her leather-knobbed high-necked jacket.

But then her gaze wavered.

'Well,' she said, 'perhaps in the circumstances I will tell you something of our future plans.'

Harriet felt a pulse of pleasure.

So, have I unexpectedly won my battle? Is this ferocious lady going to tell me what I have asked her to? And... And will that give me at least a hint, one way or the other, as to whether she is the background figure behind the break-in at Heronsgate House?

But at once a temperature-dropping thought. Can a woman like this really have used her wealth to hire thugs to make their way into Dr Lennox's office and force open that security cabinet?

Miss Tritton went over now to the long trestle table running across the whole width of the big room. For a minute or so she vigorously nosed among the papers sprawled over its surface, looking all too like the rootling blackbird Harriet had compared her to.

Then, triumphantly, she lifted up one single sheet.

'Yes,' she said. 'The draft for the Minutes of the meeting of the Council of WAGI held here on the evening of Tuesday last. A draft only, you understand. But, as it so happens, we were discussing our future plans and, as you will see, the conclusions we came to do not include any activity that even the police might construe as violent. Look, a new issue of our information pamphlet, *WAGI Wags A Finger*, letters to every Member of Parliament of whatever so-called political persuasion, and a meeting next month at the Little Theatre in Boreham.'

She thrust out the sheet.

Harriet took it, without haste, and read carefully through it. She had to acknowledge, as she finished, that it was every bit as baby-lamb innocent as Miss Tritton had claimed.

So where does this leave me? First of all, with no excuse to probe further into WAGI's activities. And second, with no further evidence whatsoever that this play-acting outfit was behind the theft of the CA 534. Sensible John is almost certainly quite right. One of the times when the sideways jump lands me in the mire.

She scanned down the list of *Those Present*.

'I see there were fifteen people at this meeting here. Do they constitute the whole membership of your Council?'

'They do,' Gwendoline Tritton said, on a note of triumph. 'So you can rest assured, Detective Superintendent, that those are our voted-for future aims.'

Harriet noted again the date of the meeting. Last Tuesday evening, the night of the break-in. Doesn't that, she asked herself, provide evidence, convincing if not infallible, that WAGI was not involved in the theft? If all its leading members were here at this house – and, look, *Meeting concluded at 12.35 a.m.* – no one from the gabbling talk-shop can have been waiting out near the Heronsgate Institute, as someone must have been, to be handed that small cardboard box Christopher Alexander described. A box that would, no doubt, have had to have been purchased with a considerable sum, half paid in advance, but half on delivery.

For a moment she tried to imagine Gwendoline Tritton, tall, eyes blinking behind big spectacles, beaky-nosed, waiting in the dark somewhere just beyond Heronsgate House, clutching a very fat bundle of used twenty-pound notes.

No, it wouldn't do.

Still, better check those fifteen names. The list could, I suppose, be a total fake.

'This is,' she asked, 'the draft copy of your Minutes?'

'It is.'

'So you must have the finished copy somewhere?'

'Of course I do. Just because you all too evidently believe WAGI is a group run by a lot of silly old women, it doesn't mean that we do not conduct our affairs in a thoroughly efficient manner. I see to that.'

I bet you do.

'So could I see that final version?'

'If you must.'

Gwendoline Tritton went, unhesitatingly, to one of the ancient wooden filing cabinets. From it she produced an impressively heavyweight Minutes Book.

It was, Harriet saw, examining it, an old-fashioned, leather-bound affair, its thick pages consecutively numbered. The Minutes for the last WAGI Council meeting had been entered, scrupulously handwritten in jet-black ink.

Nevertheless, she set the book down on a clear space on the long trestle table and carefully compared the entry to the draft copy.

Not a comma left out.

She set to then laboriously transferring to her notebook the whole of the list of *Those Present*. It would be a drag to contact each of them, but, since the loss of the CA 534 was being kept strictly secret still, it would not be a task she could pass on to a cluster of DCs.

'Oh, but wait.'

Harriet looked up.

'Yes?'

'I think I can provide a yet better guarantee of the authenticity of that list, if you care to take it up. I have just this moment recalled there is one name missing from the roll of attendees, a simple error in the notes made at the time. There present, as well as the names you have, was a lady who is, I understand, connected by marriage to your husband. She frequently pleads with us to make use of the services of the Majestic Insurance Company, though I fear I would not trust such an organisation with even tuppence ha'penny of my money. She is one Miss Beryl Farr. You can get any confirmation you need from her. I know myself how the police never accept anything they are simply told.'

Harriet had expected at that, had even looked forward to it, another tap-tap on the sternum, saying *Me, Me, I, I*. But the gesture did not come.

Outside – it was a mercifully dry day – Harriet thought over what she had learnt. She rapidly came to the conclusion that it was nothing worth knowing. Women Against Genetic Interference had every sign about it of being no more than ferocious Gwendoline Tritton's private hobby. All right, let her spend her inherited wealth in buzzing off newsletters and appeals and print-outs of significant newspaper articles to whoever came into her head. But nonetheless she was daft. No doubt about it. Daft, and only a little dangerous. If at all.

So where to go now? Back to Professor Wichmann? Or have another look at wretched Christopher Alexander? But in neither case have I any more ammunition to use. Talk to John about his Aunty Beryl, turning up once again? No point surely. He's thoroughly accounted for her as a helpless old creature.

No, nothing for it but to report to the ACC, and hope he produces some other line of inquiry. Or, perhaps even better, that he'll say there doesn't seem to be any benefit in going on with inquiries in Birchester. Or not until whoever has the CA 534 issues a threat to use it unless... Unless what? No telling.

Mr Brown saw her at once. But, in place of the sharp questions she expected about what progress she had made, he got up from behind his desk to greet her.

'Harriet, tell me about your Malcolm. Good news? Or not so good?'

She made an effort to adjust her thinking in response to that warmth, as well as to his lack of sentimentality in offering her those alternatives, *Good?* or *Not so good?*

'Well, good news really, sir. Malcolm's out of intensive care now, and he's able to talk, though he does get quickly exhausted. And then he's apt, poor boy, to think he's on the point of death, or something. But that doesn't last. He even had the courage, when we saw him last night, to ask about the group who planted that booby-trap bomb.'

'Yes. A demented lot from India, as I understand it. You know, people like that show us how these days we're all in danger. In danger of violent death coming out of nowhere, no getting past that. And for very little reason, too, that we can understand. It's something we've all got to take into account. That the weak have realised they possess the weapon of violence, senseless violence. You see it in the suicide bombers all over the world.'

One man and his bomb, the thought, even sung to that old tune, came winging back into Harriet's head.

'Yes, my husband says much the same,' she soberly answered however. 'I suppose it's all too true.'

But, at once, what he had just said made her sharply revise her decision about Women Against Genetic Interference. Wasn't that tinpot organisation one of the weak who've realised they possess the weapon of violence? If a handful of Indian hotheads could launch a murderous campaign to back their preposterous cause, so might Gwendoline Tritton and her fellow protesters.

'In fact, this brings me, sir,' she said, 'to something I

wanted to put before you.'

Then she made a face.

'Or, to be honest, to something I had decided there was no need to draw to your attention. But perhaps, I see now, that there is some need. It's a Birchester organisation called Women Against Genetic Interference.'

'Ah, I know something about them, not a great deal but something. Run by a lady by the name of – let me see – yes, Tritton, Gwen Tritton.'

'Gwendoline, in fact, sir. And spelt with a final i-n-e. I've just been interviewing her, and I don't think she'd thank you for the abbreviation.'

'You're right. She wouldn't. I met her once, and on reflection I certainly see what you mean. I can guess, too, why you changed your mind about mentioning that organisation, WAGI, as they're inclined to call themselves. They are indeed very much the sort of people I was just referring to just now. Ridiculously feeble, but therefore not unlikely to have learnt the lesson your Indian bombers have grasped, that it's all too easy to use weapons that can cause damage altogether out of proportion. All you need to make a devastating bomb, after all, is a bag of fertiliser and a little something extra. As Hasselburg has taught us all.'

'It has, sir. So, do you think I should pursue my inquiries there? I had only the merest hint that they could be behind the Heronsgate House theft, and I had thought, half an hour ago, that I could really cross them off my list.'

Mr Brown gave her a wintry Scottish smile.

'That would depend, Mrs Martens, on who else is on that list of yours, and how long it is.'

'No point in flannelling,' Harriet answered. 'My list is very short, and not very rewarding. There are just two other lines I've found to work on. There's Professor Wichmann, whom you mentioned to me, and there's a young man, Christopher Alexander, who is – or he was until a few hours ago – PA to the Director at Heronsgate House.'

'And...?'

'Right. Professor Wichmann, so I understand from DI Skelton, has been on his Special Branch files since as long ago as 1939, but that's the sole reference to him. And certainly, when I talked to Wichmann at some length, I found nothing to make me feel in the least suspicious of him. I'd put him down, in fact, as a man of simple good will, a thoroughly worthy citizen even.'

'So, what about the Heronsgate PA?'

'Well, there's a little more that's perhaps suspicious there. He was sacked from the place yesterday morning, without any warning, and, as I understand, with very little explanation. Of course, Dr Lennox may have had his reasons for believing Christopher Alexander told someone where the specimen of CA 534 was hidden, possibly reasons he couldn't quite put a finger on. But, if he suspected that was what had happened, why didn't he get in touch with you?'

'I imagine you'll know the answer, if you think for a moment about that man Lennox.'

Harriet blinked, and thought.

'Oh, yes, sir. Yes, Dr Lennox is someone who thinks he always knows best. Keeping that condemned specimen is proof enough of that.'

'Exactly, Superintendent.'

A picture of Gwendoline Tritton came into her mind then.

Another one who thinks she knows best, or believes whatever she happens to think must be so. All right, it's not at all likely that on Tuesday night an eighty-year-old lady had lurked somewhere outside Heronsgate House clutching a large sum in untraceable notes. But there could perhaps have been some trusted younger member of WAGI who could have carried out that task.

'So you think WAGI really worth digging into, sir?' she asked.

'Yes,' Mr Brown answered. 'It's likely enough, isn't it, that there was some individual at Heronsgate House who passed on the information that the Director had kept that sample of CA 543. If it wasn't his PA, it could have been someone else. How much was it common knowledge there?'

'It wasn't at all, sir. The Director – I think he knew he was acting wrongfully in keeping that specimen – was pretty careful about putting it where it was safe from any prying eyes. He eventually chose the secure filing-cabinet in his own office, a somewhat unorthodox place, but one that there was some reason to use.'

'And his PA knew he'd done that?'

'More than knew, sir. He saw him do it.'

'Very good. And were there others who knew?'

'Not directly, as I understand. But Dr Lennox did admit to me that several of his scientists could have worked out where the specimen might be.'

'He told you who those scientists were?'

'He wrote out a list of their names, sir. But, after some thought, I decided not to question any of them immediately. Dr Lennox was very concerned that nothing at all about the disappearance should get out.'

A yet more wintry Scottish smile.

'That I can well believe.'

'So you think I should interview the people on that list now, sir?'

Mr Brown sat in silence for a moment or two.

'No,' he said with a sigh. 'No, it's still worth keeping the theft a secret, though hardly for the reasons Dr Lennox may have. We don't want panic to spread through Birchester, not when we've avoided it as people here shrugged away al-Qaeda's more distant threat. No, when there are sharp newspaper types about there's every chance that bit of knowledge will be put into print if even as much as a glimmer of it gets outwith these four walls.'

'So, sir,' Harriet asked, thinking as she did that there was scarcely anyone else but the ACC to whom she would have admitted that she was floundering, 'where should I go next?'

'You've found nothing else suspicious?'

'No, sir.'

The ACC sat in silence for what seemed to Harriet several long minutes, though it could not have been anything as long.

'Harriet,' he said at last.

It gave her a small shock to hear herself addressed as such, when he had used her forename earlier only to emphasise his sincerity in asking about Malcolm.

'Harriet, when I tasked you with this inquiry I had, I ought to tell you, some doubts about whether you should be given it at this time. However, you appeared to be ready to undertake it, and I let it go forward.'

'I was ready, sir. And I still am.'

Another interval of silence.

'No, Harriet, I have to tell you that I don't think your judgment is yet on enough of an even keel.'

'But—'

'No. Let me point to one thing you said to me just now. It was when you were giving me your account of your interview with Professor Wichmann. You used words something of this order, *a man of simple good will.* But, you know, that judgment was no more than your personal feeling about the man. You had no evidence for it, none at all.'

And Harriet realised then that Mr Brown was perfectly right.

'Now,' he went on, 'I well understand how you came to feel as you did about Wichmann. Hardly more than forty-eight hours earlier you had suffered a terrible blow. Your faith in humanity, it's not too much to suppose, had been shattered. So, when you had the smallest chance of finding that faith again, you took it. I've no doubt Wichmann appears on the surface to be, as you said, a man of good will.

But what may lie below that surface?'

Harriet took a deep breath.

'Sir,' she said, 'may I go and question Professor Wichmann once more?'

'You may, Superintendent.'

Once again, Harriet, having today remembered to get herself a bite of canteen lunch, made her way up the narrow iron steps to Professor Wichmann's flat. Before pressing the familiar buzzer, she stood for a moment or two going over in her mind exactly what, on Mr Brown's instructions, she was to try to discover. Could the man seemingly filled with good will be hiding, deep inside himself, a reason for wanting to gain possession of that potentially devastating herbicide? And, if he was, what might that be? On her way to Bulstrode Road, going over and over in her mind her previous interview, she had in the end recalled a few tiny things which had not struck her then.

Hadn't there been a trace of sharpness once or twice amid the stream of jolly Germanic teasing with which he had responded to most of her questions? Had his recollections of his earliest days in Britain when his refugee father had been imprisoned as a possible spy, left him, even after all those years, with a secret anger? Or, again, hadn't there been an edge of bitterness in his confessing his hope that through Christopher Alexander he would somehow perpetuate his name in academic circles? And might that loss of a flicker of semi-immortality have turned his thoughts to revenge against an uncaring world?

Tenuous, tenuous, she thought, standing there outside the blue door, the aroma of stored potatoes from the lean-to below rising up to her.

Was Mr Brown right in saying I was careering down the wrong track in my longing for something to reassure me that goodness still existed in a world where Graham had been brutally killed, Malcolm horribly injured?

Right, let's find out, even if I have to show Professor Wichmann a very different side of myself. Let him experience what once the Hard Detective inflicted on even the pettiest wrongdoers when I was campaigning to *Stop the*

Rot.

She pressed firmly on the little white button crookedly set beside the flimsy door. From within came the crackly buzz she had heard twice before. After a minute she took her finger off the buzzer and strained forward to make out, if she could, the shuffle of approaching slippered feet.

She could not.

But perhaps he's out doing his shopping, as he was the first time I tried to see him. Or possibly now he's really fast asleep in his tall winged armchair, German book flopped on his lap.

She tried another buzz. A much prolonged one.

No response.

Tap hard, as I did before, with the tinny knocker of the letter-box? No, no good then, no good now.

Kneel and shout through the pushed-open flap?

No, give up. A word with Mr Chaudhuri down below, there among his neatly piled apples and oranges, his cunningly arranged bunches of grapes.

'Oh, no. Not at home, not at home.'

'Not here?'

Harriet could not fight down instant depression. Professor Wichmann *not at home*? Does this mean he has actually taken it into his head to make a run for it? Did my questions to him, as a few moments ago I wondered if they had, take him back to the days when his father had been interned? Has he, somewhere in his mind, got an image of two alien British police officers coming to make an arrest?

But then, like a gust of fresh air, came a wild, hilarious thought. Had neat, chubby little Mr Chaudhuri been somehow transformed into a tall, powdered-wig footman stately refusing entry to a banned visitor? *Not at home.*

The notion served, if nothing else, to bring her back to reality. If Professor Wichmann was absent from his flat, it didn't at all mean that he had, for some reason or none, disappeared. If he was not out shopping, he might well have told Mr Chaudhuri that he was spending the whole day in the university library.

'So where has he gone now?' she asked, all but producing an absent-minded professor joke.

'I am not at all knowing.'

And then she took in the anxious expression on the little greengrocer's face.

'But— But—' she stammered out.

'Yes, you are hundred per cent correct. Professor is always and always telling where he is going. So that he can be found if emergency occurs. If he is going only to university library, for shopping even, to some meeting in evening, he is telling. When he is going away also. He is leaving address, asking to have letters sent on.'

'But this time he's said nothing? Can he have forgotten? Has he done that ever?'

'No, never is he not telling.'

A sudden dreadful thought came to her.

'Mr Chaudhuri,' she said, 'do you think Professor Wichmann... That he may be there in his flat, unable to answer. Ill, or...?'

'That he has taken own life?' Mr Chauduri said firmly. 'But I am not thinking Professor was a person who would do that. All the time I am knowing, and it is now for many years, I am finding him always with a little joke when he is talking.'

But, Harriet thought, you can have had no idea that this joking old man may have been all the time mulling over the blackest of thoughts. Or that he may now be in possession of a supply of destructive CA 534.

'Mr Chaudhuri,' she said, 'you mentioned Professor Wichmann going away. Where did he go at such times? Do you know?'

'Oh, yes. Yes, I am knowing. He was going for walking. It was what he was very, very much liking. On his shoulders he would put what he was calling *my good old knapsack*. Yes, altogether very, very old, in good German leather, he was saying. And for one week, two, he would walk in beautiful

English countryside.'

'Yes. He mentioned to me that he was a devoted hiker. So, perhaps... But what I was going to ask you was: do you have a key to his flat, one you use when you are collecting his letters?'

'Yes, yes, of course I am having. In case of flood etcetera. But when he was going for walking I was not always sending on any letters.'

'No, I suppose not. However, I think it might be sensible to go up and look in at the flat.'

'One first-class idea. For some minutes I would shut up shop, and I will come also.'

But when little Mr Chaudhuri had carried his baskets of oranges, apples and neatly paired grapes inside, closed the shop and gone with Harriet round to the back, into his storage yard, up the iron steps and had then opened the blue door, they found the place unoccupied.

'All right, I must admit this puts my mind more at ease,' Harriet said, untruthfully. 'But have you any idea where he might have gone now? I mean, has he ever forgotten to let you know where he would be?'

'Never. Never.'

'Well, do you think we could take a look to see if that knapsack of his is still here? That would give us some hint about where he may be?'

'Yes, yes. I would look. He is keeping same in cupboard just here, where electricity meter is. I have seen many times.'

And the cupboard was bare. An old-style meter wheel was whirring behind its little window, and that was all. Only when Mr Chaudhuri clicked off the light switch and left the narrow hallway in darkness did it cease.

Harriet would have liked to have taken advantage of being in the flat to make a full search. But she realised she could hardly do that without arousing Mr Chaudhuri's suspicions. And if Professor Wichmann was the simple, good old man she had believed – and did still have some difficulty in not believing – then she should not, without stronger evidence, let his kindly neighbour think the old man was somehow the object of police investigation.

'Thank you, Mr Chaudhuri,' she said. 'And, yes. Here's my card with my mobile phone number. Could you call me the moment you learn anything?'

Mr Chaudhuri took the pasteboard slip, studied it intently, nodded his head with circular ambiguity. But was unambiguous in his reply.

'Oh, yes, yes. The one instant I am seeing I will be telephoning you. I also am having the mobile these days. Please do not fear.'

A thought occurred to her then.

'But does Professor Wichmann have a mobile? Can you contact him that way?'

But, even as she asked, she had to admit to herself that the combination of a state-of-the-art mobile and an aged, head-in-the-clouds professor hardly gelled.

'No, no,' Mr Chaudhuri said. 'I am not thinking Professor would be able to use such.'

'No, you're right.'

She thanked him again and plodded back to her car. Standing beside it in the faintly warm sunshine, with puffy white clouds sailing along a deep-blue sky – the promise of Spring, she thought, and my vanished hopes – she tapped out Mr Brown's number and gave him the news.

'And you say this greengrocer in the shop below is sure Wichmann has never before gone away without telling him?'

'Absolutely, sir. And I would say he's entirely reliable.'

'Very good then. I'll get in touch with those people whom I don't care to name on open air-waves, and we'll see if there's anything more they can do. And in the meantime you had better, senior officer though you are, go door-knocking and see whether anybody saw the fellow making his departure.'

'Very good, sir.'

Two hours or more of police-constable door-to-door inquiries yielded nothing.

'Good afternoon. I am a police officer making a routine inquiry.' Warrant card held up for a moment. 'Did you see, at any time today, an elderly man walking by, wearing an old leather knapsack?'

'No? Well, I'm sorry to have troubled you.'

Then next-door. 'Good afternoon, I am a police officer...' And again and again and again as the fitful sunshine grew less and less warm.

At last she had to call Mr Brown and report almost total lack of success.

'I was lucky, I suppose,' she said. 'Someone at home at all the houses I called at, bar the one right at the end of Bulstrode Road, on the corner of University Boulevard here. I'll have another crack at that later, when there may be somebody at home. But I really think we've lost all trace.'

'Can he have gone into the university campus? Isn't that possible? Be sitting there in the library, no idea what time it is?'

'No, sir. I'm actually inside the campus now. I've been making inquiries, but no dice. Just now security's extra tight all over the university. So, if he's here anywhere, someone's bound to have seen him.'

'Very good. And I can tell you that I've had no response from— From the people I mentioned.'

Silence at the other end for a second. Then the Scots-tinged voice came in her ear again.

'They're anxious to use their newest technology now. Apparently, they can trace an individual who uses a mobile phone anywhere in the whole country. Providing, of course, they have the phone's number.'

'They're unlucky then, sir. Wichmann, so the greengrocer told me, doesn't have a mobile, let alone a number for it.'

'Ah, weel.'

The Scots momentarily more evident. And, Harriet thought, the long-drawn syllable had in it a tinge of amusement.

'But, sir, you will let me know the moment they have any information of any sort?'

'You can take that as read, Superintendent.'

'So what next, sir?'

'Time off for you, Harriet. There's nothing much we can do until either we get some idea where Wichmann may be, or until – and this may happen at any moment – he issues a threat to use that stuff unless we... Well, unless I dinna know what. So, I dare say you'd like the chance to go down to London, see that wounded son of yours.'

'Thank you, sir. Yes, I would like that very much.'

John, when Harriet called him at his office, said he had phoned St Mary's earlier and had been told Malcolm was still making progress.

'So, darling, if you feel happy at going on your own, I won't come. There's a bit of a crisis here, and, if possible, I think I'd better be on hand.'

On my own.

For a moment Harriet's courage deserted her.

All right, the drive down there's no bother, and I dare say I can find somewhere to park as easily as John could. But Malcolm... To have to see him without John's steadying hand there. My once-upon-a-time little son, brother to little Graham. What will I do if he's suddenly got worse? What if he has another of those fearful pain attacks when I'm with him? What if...?

Then she pulled herself together.

'No, darling, that's quite all right,' she managed to tell John. 'Deal with your crisis, and we'll see each other at home this evening.'

'And your business? That's under control?'

'As much as it can be. Mr Brown's told me to feel free to go to London.'

'Then till tonight.'

She sat where she was in the car for a minute or two, working out what her best plan might be.

OK, no point in going directly back home now. I can get a bite of something on the way down, if I need to. And the sooner I get there, after all, the better. There's no telling what they may be doing with Malcolm, tests, another operation of some sort if he's fit enough, anything could prevent me seeing him. So I'd better get there soon as I can.

Then, just as she had re-started the engine and was making her way at walking pace to the campus exit, a thought came into her head.

Some little time's passed since I completed my door-to-door chore, and it may be possible the householder at the place on the corner of Bulstrode Road has got back home.

Go there? Or shoot off to London?

No. No use making excuses. I'm less than a hundred yards away and it'd be scarcely any trouble to turn the other way now and stop off at that house.

She nosed her way forward until the front part of the car was poking well into the broad stretch of University Boulevard. And cursed. Always likely to have heavy traffic, now a long stream of vehicles was speeding into the city.

You know, I could easily turn left here instead and zoom along to where I can safely make a U-turn and then get on the motorway on that feeder road. Damn it, if I do wait to get across here, as likely as not I'll find no one at home at that place. And I could lose hours if I stay here.

All right, not hours but—

And then for no reason that she could see there came a gap in the traffic heading into the city.

Take it, take it.

She shot forward. And, even as she got half way to the far side she realised that in the early dusk a new batch of cars was speeding towards her. She felt perspiration shoot up on her forehead.

Down hard on the pedal went her foot.

Behind her, as she swung round, there came a chorus of horn blasts.

Fuck them. I'm a police officer on duty.

She overshot the entrance to Bulstrode Road by fifty yards or more, but managed to pull in where she thought she could safely leave the car.

And at the house on the corner her ring of the bell was promptly answered.

The lady who opened the door was the type Harriet mentally called *an old dear*.

Stout in build, wrapped in a flower-print apron, feet in pom-pom pink slippers well battered by use, a dishcloth dangling from one hand, she seemed quite pleased to be answering the door even if called away from her kitchen.

But something could be about to burn there, Harriet thought.

'Good evening,' she said, quickly embarking on her spiel, 'I am a police officer making a routine inquiry. I'm sorry to disturb you at this hour, but did you happen to see, earlier today, an elderly man wearing an old leather knapsack walking past your house?'

'Oh, well, no, dear. I couldn't have done that. You see today's my baking day, so I must have been in the kitchen all morning.'

'But I did call here earlier, and got no reply.'

The old dear looked for a moment utterly astonished. Then something broke through.

'Oh, yes. Yes, you're quite right. I'd forgotten all about it. You see, my daughter rang up. She lives just three turnings along, you know, and she said her little one was poorly and she wanted to do her shopping. So I said I'd look in. Just for a minute or two. You don't like to leave a little kiddy alone like that, not when he's sick. You never know, do you?'

Harriet thought of commiserating with the old dear over the shadow of a threat that had worried her.

But she had no need to urge more talk out of her.

'And so, yes, I was out of the house for— Oh, I don't

know. Half an hour. Perhaps a bit more.'

'But while you were on your way there, or on your way back, did—'

'Well now, isn't that funny. Because I did see that old gentleman striding along as I went to Jean's, and, yes, he did have an old sort of knapsack on his back, leather you know. I quite wondered about that.'

'But when was this, Mrs— I'm afraid I didn't catch your name.'

'It's Elworthy, dear. Mrs Elworthy.'

She stood looking happily complacent, as if the acquiring of that name had been the great success of her life.

'Yes, Mrs Elworthy, and when was it you saw this gentleman?'

'Oh, it must have been quite early. I mean, my Jean does like to get her shopping done before everywhere gets too crowded. So I was on my way round there by half-past nine or a bit earlier.'

'Half-past nine. Good. And can you tell me which way the gentleman was going?'

'Oh, no, dear, you've got that quite wrong. Quite wrong. In the end I saw he wasn't walking anywhere.'

'I'm sorry, I don't quite understand.'

'He saw a bus on the far side of the road and – quite sprightly, he was – ran over and hopped on to it. It had just begun to rain again, what I call an April shower, even though it's still March. So changeable the weather now. You don't know what to wear from one day to the next.'

'No,' Harriet hastened to agree, anything to keep her informant happy to go on talking. 'I must say I like it when it's settled, when you know what's going to happen. But, tell me, where was the bus he caught going to?'

'Oh, well, to the station, of course. All the Number 17s along here end up at the station.'

So Professor Wichmann has left Birchester, almost certainly. Has left without telling tubby Mr Chaudhuri that he was going. He has fled then. Fled...where to? And why? All right, that at least is out of my hands now. Mr Brown's in touch with the Faceless Ones, and they will, I suppose, find him if he's anywhere to be found. If it isn't too late.

One man and his bomb.

Chapter Eleven

When, down in London, Harriet saw Malcolm, all her maternal fears were blown away. Although his legs were still hidden under his tent-like cover, he was propped up, ignoring the laughter-noisy television and happily reading an old Dick Francis novel.

'Mum, good to see you. And, Dad, he on his way?'

'Well, no. No, some crisis at the Majestic. So he really had to stay back there.'

'Going bust, is it, the great Majestic Insurance Company? I saw something on the TV about some other big outfit getting into trouble. Dad going to be out of a job?'

Harriet laughed.

'No, I think the Majestic's safe from pretty much anything lurking in the world of finance.'

'So poor old Dad's going to have to slave away there for years to come? Not that he does all that much slaving, if you ask me. Off to foreign parts every other month, and having who knows what sort of jolly times there. You'll find he's off with some gorgeous foreign lady one of these days.'

The faintest shadow of anxiety passed over Harriet's mind

'Now, now,' she said briskly. 'Don't knock your poor father. Even when he is off on his travels he works tremendously hard, you know.'

'Oh, yes. I do know really. Safe pair of hands, old Dad.'

'Well, you certainly seem to be much more cheerful than when we last saw you. But are things really going all right?'

'Well, yes and no, of course. Bonce all but OK, they say, and, bar a few healing cuts here and there, top half's fine. But under that tent, well, they don't seem to be able to make up their minds about things there. I asked yesterday, in fact, what were the prospects of being able to go to Graham's funeral in a wheelchair, and they did the head-shaking business. But I still hope.'

'And you really want to be there if you can?'

'Oh yes, I do. Show those Indian buggers we're not beaten yet. And – I must ask you this – is there any news about them? There's never anything on the TV. I suppose al-Qaeda's seen as more important, threatening all the time to do God knows what. But any terrorists who go about killing innocent people ought to be stopped, however few they are, however ridiculous their so-called aims. Damn it, those people could be plotting this very minute to booby trap another pair of Met officers.'

Harriet sighed.

'I'm afraid there's nothing to tell about the India's Way lot,' she admitted. 'I think Superintendent Robertson would let me know if there'd been any progress. But I haven't heard a word.'

'They want to get Sid Halley on the case,' Malcolm answered with a grin, tapping the book he had put on top of his protective tent.

Harriet had sat with him for a full half-hour before a bustling nurse came up wanting to dress his legs, and so she had to leave. In the car, as she negotiated her way through London's evening traffic, she set herself to think, not about India's Way, nor al-Qaeda, but about Professor Wichmann.

My task. That may, in fact, have been taken away from me. But it is my task still.

Did that nice old man really pull the wool over my eyes? Did he sit there in that shabby flat of his laughing to himself at this senior English police officer who was so easy to fool?

A moment then to make out what some idiot driver in a Mitsubishi was trying to do. And she let her thoughts run on again.

No, damn it, I can't believe old Wichmann did that. I am an experienced interrogator. I've seen often enough when apparently innocent people are lying their heads off. And I know he wasn't doing that.

Ease up a bit. Plod along in the near-side lane.

Yet Wichmann has gone off into the blue like that, not leaving any way of getting in touch with him, completely against his invariable practice. So why? Why's he done it? Can he, despite everything, actually have that box with the CA 534 with him? With him somewhere in England? Or somewhere in the whole of Britain? Or, damn and blast it, even somewhere outside the country?

For a few moments she imagined the old man, ancient leather knapsack on his back, leaving his flat above Mr Chauduri's shop. Yes, he would have lurked at the corner of the passage leading into Bulstrode Road until he was sure his little Indian friend wouldn't see him. Then a quick walk, even a trot, up to University Boulevard and on along it, with stout old Mrs Elworthy stumping along just behind. Then the sudden shower and, on the far side, that providential bus coming to a halt. The bus that went to Birchester Central Station, and all the rail lines radiating from it.

No. All right, main lines don't exactly radiate from Birchester Central, but they do go away from it, north and south.

An idea came into her head then.

If the professor left, as Mrs Elworthy could vouch for, at about half-past nine, what would be the next train he would catch? Because I'm fairly certain that a man as precise as Wichmann would have planned his departure for exactly the train he would take.

Curse it. Can't possibly work this any further until I get back.

Oh, yes, I can.

With a fine disregard for best driving practice, she reached for her mobile and rang John.

He answered at once.

'John, it's Harriet. Where are you?'

'Just got home.'

'Then there's something you can do for me. Could you

look up long-distance trains leaving Birchester soon after, say, ten this morning?'

'Well, I could. But why? And where are you, come to that?'

'Oh, I'm on my way home now, be on the motorway any minute. But I'd like to check on those trains as soon as possible. It's a work matter.'

'All right, if you say so. I won't pry, I can take a hint. But I'll need a few minutes to find the rail timetable or ring the station. I'll call you back.'

'John, thank you.'

'Oh, and one thing.'

'Yes?'

'When I do call, bring the car to a neat halt on the hard shoulder or wherever and then answer.'

'Yes, sir. Very good, sir.'

She was well on the motorway before her mobile played its little tuneless tune, and she decided to ignore that husbandly advice.

'Yes?' she snapped out, speeding along.

'All right, you can't stop, for some reason or other. So I'll be quick. There was the ten-fifteen going right up north, as far as Windermere, though you have to change at Preston. Then no main-line departures after that until an eleven o'clock London express, which goes on past there, all the way on down to Brighton. A good few departures earlier than ten, but nothing afterwards till the train going to Preston.'

'John, you're a marvel.'

And so am I, in my way, she thought as she cut the call. Off goes Professor Wichmann apparently into the blue, and – when eventually I think of this – I track that walking enthusiast from long ago in the Schwartzwald of Germany, to— Yes, right to Windermere, bang in the middle of the walking country of the Lake District.

But will he just be walking there? Or will he be looking for a suitable place to experiment with CA 534 before he issues a threat to use it?

But it still could be that my own inquiries scared an innocent old man, who was once a very young man living in a country where the threat of arrest, merely for one's racial origins, always lurked. Was it me who made him, scared by that police interest, suddenly go into hiding?

But, whatever the reason, he has disappeared. And he still has to be found. So, call Mr Brown with my deduction?

Well, better not. Better wait a little until I've gone over all this and made sure it's watertight. And better to wait, too, to use the mobile when I'm no longer driving.

Back home, however, she had seen nothing to doubt in her reasoning. Or, at least, she felt her notion was still worth pursuing, though, late as it was, she postponed ringing Mr Brown with a mere notion.

When, first thing next day, she did call him, having waited since it was Sunday to give him time to be up and about, he agreed that her theory was worth pursuing. If with some expressions of Scottish caution. 'We'll see, though,' he concluded. 'We'll see if those unmentionables down there in London come up with something first.'

Harriet realised then that she had come to the end, for the time being, of her inquiries. The man whom the Faceless Ones had put in the frame, with the merest fragment of evidence only, that single reference in Inspector Skelton's files, was the subject of a full-scale hunt. Her share in it, for what it had been worth, was now over. All right, with no mobile, Wichmann can't be pinpointed among the Cumbrian hills, where I believe him to be. But that doesn't mean that he can't be found. Perhaps even more easily there than elsewhere because there are so few people at this time of year out on those bleak but beautiful mountainsides. So, sooner or later, he will be traced. Traced and arrested.

Then will I have to go up to Windermere, or wherever they take him, to confront him in a cell? Or will that task be given over lock, stock and barrel to the Faceless Ones?

Sitting there after breakfast – John had fetched fresh

croissants – she asked herself: what do I do now?

Answer: sit here like a lemon.

A lemon, she suddenly thought, that's oozing tears. Tears for dead Graham, tears for Malcolm, perhaps never to walk again. Yes, Mr Brown's recommendation of work as the way to drag oneself out of the worst of grief has abruptly been, if not withdrawn, at least put into suspension. And what has happened? Grief has come tumbling back.

Graham. My Graham. My newcomer to the service, guardian of my belief in it, is dead. His life all in one second ended by the unthinking actions of a few deluded terrorists.

She turned to John, sitting ploughing through the massed pages of the *Sunday Times*.

'John, John. What is happening to the world? Has everything changed for ever? Graham's dead. Do you realise that? He's dead. Dead, dead.'

John let the paper fall in a heap to the floor, rose to his feet, crossed over to her, stooped and put a hand on her shoulder.

'Darling, no, the world hasn't changed. And, yes, I do realise Graham's dead. That's been there solidly in the back of my mind ever since that phone call from Notting Hill police station. But I've been lucky, in a way. At much the same time things in the office began to go haywire. A senior executive – no names, of course – was suspected of having his hand in the till, deep in. It's the sort of possibility that hovers over all concerns dealing in huge sums. Well, now it looks as if he really is guilty. Looks, but no more. We'll see. Still, the effect of all the hoo-hah has been that I just haven't been able to think much about what happened to us.'

He gave her arm a reassuring squeeze.

'Listen, I know it's early morning, but why don't we have a drink? Or... Or shall we go back up to bed?'

'No. No, not that. I couldn't bear to. I couldn't bear to think of that sort of happiness when... When Graham... You know, ever since we heard I haven't...'

'And you know that, lying awake far into the night, I haven't either.'

She looked up.

'But, yes. A drink would help. It only really all came back fully into my mind because, quite suddenly, the task Mr Brown gave me has gone into suspension. Then the black thoughts swept in.'

She took hold of the large whisky and ginger he made for her – she'd noted the spirit splashing into the glass, the ginger ale spurting up as the bottle was opened.

'So here I am,' she said, 'with nothing to do. And I don't like it.'

John, head down at the little fridge they had in the corner, looking for a bottle of his Australian chardonnay, muttered something she only just caught.

'When there's nothing to be done, do nothing.'

'Do nothing?' she snapped as soon as what he had said sank in. 'But you can't just sit there and decide there's nothing to be done. Not when there is something, however hard it is to see what to do about it next.'

John straightened up, bottle in hand.

'Well, that's my philosophy,' he said. 'And I haven't found it altogether a bad way of looking at things.'

He took the corkscrew out of its drawer and began opening the chardonnay

'As a matter of fact,' he said over his shoulder, 'now I come to think about it, I have got something for you to do.'

'All right, anything to keep me occupied.'

'Well, maybe you'll withdraw that offer, when you hear what it is. You see, I don't like to be out of touch with my fellow board members just at the moment. It's possible, just, that I may be called in, Sunday or no Sunday.'

'Well, come on, what's this leading up to?'

He produced the hint of a grin.

'To you going in my place for my long overdue Sunday visit to Aunty Beryl.'

'But I've never met the woman, and she's your aunt or

cousin or whatever, so—'

She came to a halt.

True enough, she said to herself, I don't see any good reason to pay John's distant cousin a call in his stead. But I do know something about her. She's a member of the Council of WAGI. And, all right, WAGI, despite Mr Brown's thoughts on violence as the weapon of the weak, has never looked to me likely as the Heronsgate House culprit. But, if eventually it turns out old Wichmann has some perfectly good reason for suddenly vanishing, then WAGI, however hopeless an outfit it is, does come back into play. Sort of.

'OK,' she said to John. 'There is actually something I'd intended at one stage to check with your aunt or cousin or whatever. So I might as well do it now. So, as seeing her will keep me nicely occupied for an hour or two, and occupation seems to be a good thing, I'll go. Even if it is you just dodging out of it.'

'I'm not actually. I may get a call from the Chairman at any moment.'

'Take your word for it. So when shall I be off? I suppose I'd better get her a bunch of flowers or something.'

John looked for an instant mortified.

'Do you know,' he said, 'I've never, in all the years I've brought myself to visit the old— Well, the word *bitch* sprang into my mind. But shall I say *in all the years I've been visiting the old lady* I never thought to take her flowers. They didn't seem to fit the image, somehow.'

'Well, bitchy image or no bitchy image, I'm going to do the right thing and take flowers. I see a bunch of Spring-yellow daffodils. A great big bunch.'

She went at four o'clock, the established time for John's infrequent Sunday visits, since there was no way of letting Beryl know she was coming. 'Heavens no,' John had said when she had suggested giving her a call in advance, 'the old creature hasn't had a phone for years, says she can't afford it, even though I actually offered to foot the bill.'

The flat, when she rang the bell in the centre of its ill-painted brown door, proved to be every bit as awful as John had once said it was, and Aunty Beryl looked as if she might be just as difficult, even bitchy, as he had said.

She was a shrivelled up old lady of, Harriet guessed, seventy-five or so. Thin in every part of her, stick legs in what looked like lisle stockings, wrinkled here and there, a body, under an ancient woollen dress in two shades of blue, both pale, more like a skeletal collection of bones than a creature of flesh and blood, and a narrow, sunken face yet more wrinkled than the stockings. Only from out of it there darted a pair of active blue eyes.

The flat – Harriet had been struck at once by a faint, pervasive odour of urine – was even shabbier than Professor Wichmann's. The only two armchairs in its single tiny living-room were grimed over and worn down to the threads of their covers, almost impossible to guess what colours or pattern there had once been. There was a small carpet, perhaps better called a mere rug, and Harriet, as she took it in, made a quick mental note not to trip on any of the holes she spotted. The gas fire, not lit although the day was blustery and cold, had next to it, almost as big, a bright-red meter menacingly demanding coins for its maw.

'I don't suppose you remember me,' she had said in greeting, 'though you were at our wedding, all those years ago. I'm Harriet, John's wife. He's been terribly busy at the office all this weekend, I'm afraid, some crisis or other. So I've come in his place.'

Scarcely pausing, in view of the fiercely suspicious look in Aunty Beryl's button-blue eyes, she thrust forward the big double bunch of daffodils.

'I— I brought these for you.'

Aunty Beryl, with a new look of suspiciousness, seized hold of them and banged them down, as if they were laden with some deadly poison, on the narrow, ornately carved mahogany sideboard taking up almost the whole of one of the walls of the cramped little room.

'Oh, yes,' she said, her slight Birchester nasal twang manifesting itself, 'I know who you are. Always getting your picture in the *Evening Star*. Or you were in the days when I used to see it. Don't get it any more. Nothing but wickedness in it: rapes, violence, drunks reeling about the streets, stalkers, everything. A body doesn't feel safe, not for a moment.'

Harriet had felt depression creeping up ever since she had heard the bolts on that battered front door being pulled back one by one and the door itself at last opened, scraping over a loose piece of floor-covering in the tiny hallway. She managed now to fight off her gloom with a mental poor-taste joke about the unlikelihood of anybody wanting to rape Aunty Beryl.

'Yes,' she said, 'the *Star* likes nothing better than to print a picture of me when some investigation's not going well. But it's something I have to put up with.'

But Aunty Beryl was not made any sweeter by that.

'And your twin boys,' she had gone spitting on, 'the one killed, the other in hospital and not likely to come out of it. I heard about them on my little radio, in spite of not seeing the *Star* and not having that nasty television.'

That mention of the twins hurt. For a moment, to keep herself in control, Harriet had to stand there in silence, biting at her lower lip.

At last she managed to say something.

'Well, I'm happy to say that Malcolm, the one in hospital, is getting better every day. The doctors don't say anything about— About his not being able to leave eventually, though they're not sure he'll be able to go to Graham's funeral, even in a wheelchair. But otherwise the outlook isn't too bad.'

'There's that MSA, remember,' Aunty Beryl came back. 'They say every hospital's riddled with it nowadays. Nasty little germs all over everywhere. Deadly when you do catch one. Deadly. Nothing they can do. One reason I hope I'll never have to end my days in hospital, not wherever it is, that St Oswald's here or St Mary's down in London. They're all the same. More dying of MSA than of what they've been taken in for.'

Again Harriet had to force herself to thrust away what the old woman was saying. Or direly prophesying.

The best she could do was to correct her, and not without sharpness.

'I think you must mean MRSA, not MSA,' she said. 'I'm not sure what all the letters stand for, but the R is *resistant*. To antibiotics, I think.'

She nerved herself up to declare that Malcolm was very unlikely to be affected in that way. But, even as she thought it, she realised it was by no means as impossible as she was about to assert.

She clamped her lips shut.

And then, at the last moment, a quick idea came to her. Perhaps even a useful one.

'Yes,' she said, jabbering a little, 'everything seems to be initials these days, don't you think? DVDs, VHS – Oh, I don't know – FIFA and BAFTA, OAPs and OBEs. Who knows what they all stand for? Didn't John, in fact, tell me you yourself belonged to something called W-A-G-I?'

'Women Against Genetic Interference,' Aunty Beryl proclaimed, drawing herself up.

'Ah, yes. That was it. Have you been a member long?'

'For years. A friend of mine from the old days, Gwendoline Tritton, asked me to join. We do very good work, you know. People just don't realise what terrible things scientists are up to nowadays. Changing everything they set their eyes on. The food we grow, all the animals, making them quite different just to suit their own ideas, even altering human beings. Clonging. Clonging.'

'Yes,' Harriet said, deciding not to offer *cloning*.

And how could you explain to someone like Aunty Beryl – perhaps to any WAGI member – that they were caught up in a whirlwind of wild exaggeration?

Yes, I can see now why John keeps putting off visiting

her, if he gets a stream of such utterly illogical ideas flung at him whenever he opens his mouth, let alone the envious insults. All right, one ought to feel sorry for anyone living like this, poor as poor, when once – at the time of our wedding? – she must have been reasonably comfortably off. Now here she is, afraid of being mugged, of ending her days in a germ-infested hospital, of the *nasty* television and a dozen other things. A miserable life. But, when seeing her means exposing oneself to the sort of unpleasantness she's just flung at me, it'd be by no means easy to do the decent thing and come to Sunday tea. Not that I've been offered a cup, for all those daffodils I brought.

Chapter Twelve

Despite the sharp chill in the air, Harriet, who had left Aunty Beryl's wretched flat at the end of another half hour almost as if she was fleeing from the plague, stood just where she was on the stained and sticky pavement, just round the corner out of sight of Beryl's windows. She breathed deeply in.

God, I'm glad to be out of that. And was it in any way worthwhile? Did I learn anything more about WAGI as Aunty Beryl went on spitting and snarling with whatever came next into her head as I tried to chat? Well, yes, I suppose, I did. A bit. A tiny bit. I managed to gather that WAGI's a more active organisation than I learnt from those Minutes that Gwendoline Tritton flourished in my face, that it meets quite frequently, sends out a lot of propaganda.

Even though Aunty Beryl suddenly clammed up, I learnt that they still occasionally like to inflict a little physical damage, more than that single attack on the crop of GM maize that earned fines for those taking part, Aunty Beryl's paid by John.

But did I learn anything indicating that WAGI, rather than old Professor Wichmann, had managed to hire the thugs who petrol-threatened that blarneying Irishman, Michael O' Dowd? And, no, I didn't. It's impossible to believe a lot of old women could have the knowledge or contacts to get hold of criminals like the ones who used such violence. Ferocious though Gwendoline Tritton is, I just can't see anyone like her being able to do that.

Nor, come to that, do I see old Wichmann knowing where to find any criminal heavies. Unless... Unless, still hard to believe, he's all along had contacts with some relic Nazi organisation. That all his talk of living under threat in Germany before the Second World War was pulling the wool over my innocent eyes.

Then a nasty little forgotten task came back to her.

Oh God, I never asked damned Beryl if she had been at the Council meeting of WAGI on the night of the raid, if she could vouch for all fifteen members, sixteen with herself, being there till after midnight.

Go back and see her again? Be assaulted with jibes about Graham and Malcolm? No. No, I absolutely can't.

But never mind that I still haven't questioned the other names on that list. No point now, really, now that Wichmann's disappeared.

She shrugged her raincoat more closely round herself and set off to where she had left the car.

So it is, as Dad used to say, *home James*. And still, thanks to the Faceless Ones taking the hunt for Wichmann totally under their control, with nothing to do.

There at home over their evening drinks she managed with some difficulty not to tell John – no call from his crisis-hit Chairman – why she had really gone to Aunty Beryl. No reason to tell him any more about the missing CA 534 than he had already known. But tell him about his cousin or aunt she must.

'All right,' she burst out in answer to his mildly interested inquiry, 'you really let me in for it there, didn't you? I mean, the decent thing would have been to have given me some warning. But, no. You just let me be trapped in that appalling flat in sleazy Moorfields—'

'Oh, come on,' John interrupted. 'I know Moorfields has its unlovely aspects, but Harrington Street isn't too bad.'

'And when were you last there to know how bad it is?'

Mustn't take out my rage on poor John. But, damn it, I've got to vent it on somebody.

John raised both hands, palms outwards, in defence.

'Well, all right, it has been perhaps six months since I saw Beryl. But I still think there are worse places round there than Harrington Street.'

'Maybe there are. But what you never really told me before I went off was what she's actually like.'

John smiled.

Weakly, she thought.

'Well, you know,' he said, 'if I'd given you the complete character study, good side and bad, you wouldn't ever have gone there, would you?'

'What *good side*, for heaven's sake?'

'Oh, she does have some good qualities. She may be a little bitter nowadays, and who can blame her, forced to live the life she does. But in the old days she was no more than a bit of a busybody. And, you know, busybodies, though they can be a pain, do have their good points. When they interfere, they often manage to do some good to somebody.'

'Well, she didn't do me any good, I can tell you that.'

John looked at her carefully, and then evidently decided it was safe to speak.

'Actually, she did do you some good. When you left for Moorfields you were in a pretty depressed state. I could see that. But now you seem to be fighting fit, even if it is your long-suffering spouse that you're fighting.'

'Oh, no, you don't get out of it with fancy arguments like that.'

She paused and took a deep breath.

But then it occurred to her that what John had said wasn't exactly a fancy argument. All right, I do feel better now than I did when I left home. So I suppose seeing that old harridan did do me some good. And... And I sort of feel it did me more good than just making me be horrid to John. Can't think why, but...

'All the same,' she went on, rather less heatedly, 'you did send me into the lion's mouth, or lioness's mouth if you like, totally without warning. Do you know what she said to me when I'd hardly got into that awful room of hers? She actually spewed out her envy and hatred of the world and all that's in it by saying, without a word of regret, she knew Graham had been killed and Malcolm injured. She brought it out, just like that.'

'Yes. Yes, well, all right, perhaps I should have told you what to expect. But even I wouldn't have been prepared for her to be as heartless as that.'

'Well, she was.'

'But, just consider this, you've just been able to tell me what she said, her very words. But, when we were talking after breakfast this morning, one single passing thought about the boys sent you tumbling down into black grief and despair.'

She took stock.

'Yes,' she said after a moment or two, 'you're quite right. Somehow, perhaps it was even because of that beastly woman, I do feel now a little more able to cope. John, do you think, though, that's right? I mean, here it is Sunday, less than a week since we were talking about the threat of far-off thunder and that terrible phone call came, and shouldn't I still be devastated by grief?'

John looked across at her from where he was sitting.

'I don't really think there's any *should* about it,' he said. 'What's right, I think, is just what you feel at any moment. I'm sure that there'll be times, not only in the days leading up to next Tuesday, but for months to come, years even, when the impact of it all strikes again, just as violently as it did as we went careering down to London that first time to see Malcolm with you sat beside me there hunched in utter misery.'

'So, it's OK if I don't sit here in tears all the time?'

'Yes, I truly believe it is, especially as you're undertaking Mr Brown's hard-work remedy for grief. So, you can tell me now what other news you gathered about Aunty Beryl?'

'If I must.'

She shook her head clear.

'Right, well, there wasn't much. Let me see. Yes, she's given up reading the *Star*.'

'So have you.'

'True, and she's probably right to have done it as well. After all, who wants daily doses of rape and— Oh, John, I must tell you. When she was complaining that the *Star* was filled with nothing but accounts of the appalling things she saw as threatening her, she headed the list with rape, and I couldn't help joking to myself that of all unlikely rape victims your Aunty Beryl was the safest.'

John gave a brief chuckle of a laugh.

'Yes, that's hardly news to me. Poor old thing, she never was, as far as I can make out, much of a target for ravening males, and I can't see her being a victim now, however often the *Star* has its *Woman of 154 Assaulted in Own Home* stories.'

'Yes. That's the thing. She does have a hard life, a horribly hard one, tell the truth, but she also makes the most of her hardships, the most and a bit more. So you, for one, put off visiting her, and I declare here and now that I won't ever see her again.'

'OK, I promise I'll take over from now on and assuage – if that's the word – my long held guilt.'

Harriet felt she had made her point.

And something else, something more, seemed to have been planted now at the back of her mind, though she was unable, scratch at it as she would, to free it from the depths of her unconscious. A little irritating scab.

The scab, if scab it was, ceased altogether to itch early next morning. Harriet's mobile rang while she was still reading the papers after breakfast and cursing things in general because she still had nothing to do. John had told her the night before that it would be ridiculous, and even dangerous, for her to ask to go back to her regular duties at least until after the funeral.

'You aren't fit to assume responsibilities,' he'd said. 'All right, at this moment you feel you are, but you know what it is; quite suddenly, without any warning or real cause, you'd be overwhelmed by misery and grief. You know you would. Come to that, I might well be myself. I've been on the edge of it more than once. But, if it happened to me, I could drop what I was doing and no great harm would come of it. The Majestic always takes its time. But with you and police work it's not the same thing. All right, you've been active these past few days. But you've had your Mr Brown backing you up every inch of the way. So, now, you must content yourself with slowly trying to get back to a steadier state. You know what I say: when there's nothing to be done, do nothing.'

'OK.'

It had been all she could manage.

But now suddenly her mobile was singing its little, alarming song.

She recited her number.

'Harriet? Andrew Brown.'

Coincidence, when John's just pointed to him as my safeguard? Or, in fact, is it father figure just being fatherly?

'Yes?'

'Something I'm going to tell you, off the record. Something that, strictly, I shouldn't be mentioning at all.'

'Yes...?'

'It's this. We have had an ultimatum. From whoever has the CA 534. They don't, of course, identify themselves, but there's been a letter simply stating that, unless steps are immediately announced to stop research into genetically modified foods, areas of the countryside will be razed by a certain highly persistent herbicide, I quote, "now in our possession". Very well, I would like your view on that.'

It did not take Harriet more than a second to know what her view was.

'It's WAGI,' she said. 'It can't be anyone else, however unlikely they look as an effective organisation. But genetically modified foods are their big thing. And it's always been in my mind that they'd have given their eye-teeth to have got hold of the CA 534, though God knows how a tinpot lot like that has done it. But, never mind, it's exactly the sort of threat they'd like to be holding over the country.'

'I understand what you mean. However, that was not the

response of the people at the Home Office, where the letter arrived first thing this morning. They're in touch with the people I prefer not to name, and their advice doesn't deviate by an inch from the belief that your fugitive Professor Wichmann is the man responsible.'

'And do you... Well, is that your view of it, too?'

'I am calling you, Harriet,' came the give-nothing-away Scottish voice.

She thought rapidly about all the implications. The theft of the CA 534 is now a definite threat to the whole economy of the country, especially if whoever has it gets to learn how heat treatment can make it multiply so fast. So it's right that the Faceless Ones should be in full charge of the hunt for Professor Wichmann, if it's him who issued that ultimatum. But Andrew Brown doesn't hold that view, however little he contrives to admit it in words of one-syllable. So can I, should I, do what my instincts tell me is right? Go along a hundred per cent with my boss?

Answer. Damn it, yes.

'So what do you think I should be doing?' she asked.

A tiny chuckle of satisfaction at the far end.

'I don't think it would be altogether a bad thing, Superintendent, if, from strictly a security angle, you were to look into the activities of a certain group that goes by the name of WAGI.'

'Search that house, The Willows? I'd need a team, of course.'

'So you would. But I think a search would be a wee bit premature. It would only alarm them, if they should be the people we want, and we'd not be very likely to find anything that easily. No, just a visit, I think, Harriet. A morning call.'

'Very good. I'll make it that.'

Right, she thought, it's no longer *when there's nothing to be done, do nothing.*

Her mobile rang again almost as soon as she had put it away.

Cautious Mr Brown already countermanding the order

he's taken care not to give me in so many words? But her caller was someone else, and altogether unexpected.

'Detective Superintendent Martens?' a hesitant male voice asked.

'Speaking.'

'You— You gave me your mobile number. You said if— If there was anything else I thought of—'

She could bear it no longer.

'Who are you?'

'Oh. Oh, yes. Yes, I haven't said.'

'Well?'

'It's Christopher Alexander. You know, it was me you—'

'Yes, yes. I know who you are. Now, tell me why you're calling me.'

She could hear the gulp coming all the way through the air.

'I— I— Well, I think there's something I ought to— Well, to confess.'

Harriet hauled all her patience into play.

'Just tell me what it is that's troubling you,' she said. 'And then we'll see if there's anything that ought to be done about it.'

Another gulp on the radio waves.

'Well, you see, what it is, is this. I— I suddenly thought last night – I was sort of lying awake, you know – and I suddenly realised that I— That I might have, without meaning to, told— Well, told my girlfriend, er, Maggie, you know...'

Maggie? Maggie? What the hell's her proper name? Can't remember. But better let him go on. If I don't, he may clam up altogether.

She imagined Christopher's Maggie, beside him on that mattress on the floor of his flat, when he had let slip...something.

'All right, Christopher,' she said, 'you think you mentioned something you shouldn't have to your Maggie. What was it?'

'Well, I'm not quite sure what I did say. But— But I think I may have said something about the CA 534. About what exactly it is, and how important my work at Heronsgate House was. I— Well, you see, she, Maggie, was sort of— Well, knocking me. She said I was a weakling. I mean, she's very athletic herself, you know, and— Well, she went on to say I was only a kind of office boy and Heronsgate House was just a minor research place. So I— Well, I told her how important my work really was, and how – I think I said this – there was the CA 534 in the Director's filing cabinet and that he and I were the only people who knew about it.'

'I see. But you're not certain you actually said to Maggie— What's her surname, by the way? It always helps to know that. If only to sort her out from all the other Maggies.'

Not, she thought fiercely, that there are so many girls with that name these days. But I must know exactly who she is if this wretched young man did really tell her where Dr Lennox hid that CA 534 sample. Because she could... But let's hear who she is.

'Oh, it's Quirke.'

Of course, Quirke.

'All right, now just quietly think again about that conversation you had with her. Where were you when you were talking? That's always a good way to bring things back to mind.'

'I was— Well— Well, we were sort of in bed together, actually.'

'OK, it's not a criminal offence to go to bed with a girl. So, now, just what did you say to her? After you'd made it clear your job was important, what exactly did you go on to say about Dr Lennox?'

'Yes, yes. That was it. I was saying how he had to rely on me for some things, and that he wasn't without faults. And then, yes. Yes, I did say he'd just put the CA 534 into his security cabinet.'

'And that was all?'

'Yes, yes, I'm sure it was. And does it matter really that I just mentioned it to her? I mean, I'm sure she forgot as soon as I said it. Well, actually, I'm sort of sure she did. Because, well, straight after that she—Well, she began to make love again. So she must have got a better opinion of me, mustn't she?'

'I'm sure she did, Christopher. And you mustn't worry about that little slip of yours. Don't, of course, mention it to anybody else, particularly not to your *Evening Star* friend Tim Patterson. But otherwise just forget all about it.'

But, she thought tucking the mobile away, I am not going to forget about it. Because didn't that same Tim Patterson tell me that Maggie Quirke was a member of WAGI?

So, yes, let the Faceless Ones go hunting all over the Lake District for Professor Wichmann. I'm surprised they haven't found him yet. But I am going to do what Mr Brown so cautiously suggested and go to see Miss Gwendoline Tritton once again to find out, if I can, whether it did occur to that young WAGI member to pass on her interesting piece of information to the organisation's chairman. Or does she insist on being called its Chair?

Chapter Thirteen

Gwendoline Tritton came to the door herself when Harriet rang the bell at The Willows. She looked exactly as she had done at their last meeting, right down to the faded blue trainers on her large feet.

'You again,' she said with all her old ferocity.

Harriet simply stood there.

'Yes, it's me, Detective Superintendent Martens. I have some more questions about the activities of WAGI.'

'Do you? And what if I will not answer? You'd arrest me, I suppose. Then let me tell you it won't be the first time that I've been in police custody. I told them nothing then, and I won't tell you anything now. However much pressure you bring to bear.'

Good heavens, the woman really must be mad, or very nearly so. To loose off like that at the mere sound of my name. She's hysterical.

Then another thought came.

Hysterical, or pretending to be so? If she has really got something to hide, it could be a way of making me think she's not worth investigating and nor is her WAGI. But, if Maggie Quirke did pass on what she learnt from poor wavering Christopher, then it's more than likely that the letter threatening to unloose CA 534 unless work on genetically modified foods is brought to an end was written at the work-station beside that long table in the former drawing-room just inside here. And I'm going to do my damnedest to discover if it was.

Oh, for the days of the vanished typewriter and its give-away chipped *e*'s or missing tails to its *g*'s.

'Miss Tritton,' she said, 'there is no reason at all for you to take this attitude. WAGI, like any other organisation, has a duty, if questions about its work and aims have arisen, to answer them. So, may I please come in and put those questions to you, as WAGI's chairman.'

'Chair, Chair, Chair,' Miss Tritton shouted.

'Very well, as WAGI's Chair, if that's what you prefer.'

And Gwendoline Tritton abruptly succumbed.

'Oh, come in then. Come in, if you must.'

Harriet followed her into the big ground-floor room, stiffening herself, as she entered, not to cast a glance at the work-station. Somehow she felt that if she did look at it for some unlikely trace that there had rested there in the tray of its printer the ultimatum to distant high-in-the-heavens Whitehall, she would fail in her quest.

She pushed the superstition out of her mind.

'Miss Tritton,' she said, 'we have been considering the facts I learnt about WAGI on my previous visit here and we are not altogether satisfied that your activities do not now go beyond the legal limits. You must be aware that, in view of the terrorist threat to the country as a whole, changes have been made to the laws. Some of the freedoms the ordinary citizen has traditionally possessed have been curtailed in the interests of the safety of us all.'

'In the interests of the beasts and the bureaucrats who would like to make us all their slaves,' Miss Tritton came fighting back.

'That's your view,' Harriet said, 'and you are perfectly entitled to hold it.' She let a tiny pause hang in the air, and then added 'unless you have carried it beyond words and into actions.'

Apparently she had made that seem threatening enough to give the ferocious WAGI Chair something to think about. For several seconds she stood there, compressing her lips into a tight line of opposition.

'And what have we done that makes you think so?' she asked eventually.

'That's what I have come here to learn.'

At this Gwendoline Tritton's lips curled upwards into a thin smile.

A smile that said *catch me if you can*.

'When I was here before,' Harriet began, feeling herself

like a cat, belly to the ground, inch by inch approaching this strong-beaked blackbird, 'you were good enough to show me the Minutes of your most recent Council meeting. There was, as I remember, an item listing future activities. I wonder if you could find a copy and go through it telling me which of those projects have been implemented, and with what outcomes?'

Miss Tritton thought. Harriet could almost see the process running through her mind. Safe to show the Minutes again to this persistent police officer? Or not? What had been in them?

'Very well,' she said at last. 'I can see no objection to that.'

Damn, Harriet thought, she's calculated there's nothing there conceivably leading to that ultimatum letter. My blackbird has hopped out of claw-reach.

But, handed the heavy black-bound Minutes Book now, she had to look through that entry for Tuesday, March 16. She did her best to find something that hinted at any illegal activity, but there was nothing under the *Future Activities* item that gave her the least toe-hold. *Members Present?* Yes, inserted there now there's *Miss B Farr*, Aunty Beryl, and with an addition. Left meeting at 8.06 p.m. Yes, didn't John say something about her not liking to be out late at night? Very precise minute-keeping at WAGI. Oh, and, now that I know the surname, here's *Miss M Quirke* too, Christopher's girl and actually a member of WAGI's Council.

So ask about her?

At once a better thought.

No. If I say anything to Gwendoline Tritton that shows I know about the secret Maggie Quirke may have got out of Christopher – deliberately or just by chance in the course of a lovers' tiff – then it will alert this formidable old woman. So, look for some other opportunity.

But isn't this in any case one more indication that WAGI could have the CA 534 in its possession? Because if

Maggie's a full Council member, rather than just some hanger-on, as I had thought up to now, can't I see her standing in the dark outside Heronsgate House, a large wad of twenty-pound notes in her hand, waiting to pay for a small cardboard box just taken from Dr Lennox's security cabinet? Much more likely her than aged Gwendoline Tritton.

So have I found out all I need to know?

Then, abrupt descent of hopes. No, damn and blast it. What I'm looking at is in fact the very evidence that Maggie cannot have been there for that hand-over. There's the simple statement here at the end of the page, *Meeting concluded at 12.35 a.m.*, that infantile boast about how long it went on, how important were its discussions. But nonetheless evidence, and reasonably good, that the hand-over of that box, if it took place at all, was not made immediately after the break-in which happened shortly before midnight.

All right, it's possible that one of those criminal heavies came here next day with the box and went away with pockets stuffed with money. But it's pretty unlikely. Gwendoline Tritton would have expected the break-in to be reported as soon as it was discovered, which, thanks to those two inept Birchester Watchmen, it was not. She would then never have risked a visitor of that sort being seen at The Willows.

So, not-so-clever Harriet. All I've done by coming here is to make the case against WAGI that much less convincing. And in the meanwhile, perhaps, the Faceless Ones have found Professor Wichmann and even got a confession out of him.

It had been an embarrassing ten minutes getting away from Gwendoline Tritton and that long trestle table. She had had to produce duff questions such as what was the agenda for the forthcoming meeting at the Little Theatre in Boreham. 'I shall,' Miss Tritton had answered, tapping her breastbone, 'be addressing the meeting myself and taking questions, but no more.' Then, more desperately, she had asked if the next issue of *WAGI Wags A Finger* had gone out, and who, if anyone, the finger had been wagged at.

Eventually she had got away, conscious that, as she had turned to take a last look at the tall façade of the big house, its chimney stacks ranged against pale blue, almost wintry sky, WAGI's ferocious Chair had drawn herself up at the door in full triumph.

In the car she had driven off a short way and then used her mobile to report to Mr Brown what she had been told by Christopher Alexander, and how what had looked a likely way forward with WAGI had ended in complete lack of success.

Will he think I'm not really up to the task he's given me, she had asked herself, as she dabbed at the numbers.

'All right, Harriet,' his dry answer came, 'we can't expect to beat our friends from London as easily as that. And, forbye, they may be the ones on the right track, rather than us. Not that they've located their professor yet, so I gather.'

'Have you any suggestions how I can get at WAGI some other way, sir? Should I get hold of this Maggie Quirke and see if she's a softer target than Gwendoline Tritton?'

'She'll be there when we want her, Harriet. And perhaps we should give the hunters on the Cumbrian hills a wee while longer. So, go home now. I dare say you'll want to visit young Malcolm again this afternoon.'

'Yes. Yes, thank you.'

She drove away, too depressed at the prospect of *nothing to do* once more to pay much attention to where she was going.

So it came as a slight surprise to see that the vehicle ahead of her was a double-decker bus moving at a good speed along a wide main road.

Jesus, where am I? What's the number of that bus? Can't see from the rear. Oh, right, yes. Yes, I can. It's a 17. Now, where…?

Can't think.

Oh, yes, I can, though. The 17s go to Birchester Central Station. Fat Mrs Elworthy told me so when she saw old Wichmann making his getaway. Not that this one ahead is going to the station. It's on its way from there to— I don't know. It's pulling up at a stop now, though. Perhaps when I've gone past I'll—

It was then, just as she began to pull out, that she saw a familiar figure getting down from the bus. An old, white-haired man with, on his back, an ancient leather knapsack.

She brought the car to a screeching halt, its rear still half-slewed out into the road, flung off her seat-belt, slid across the passenger-seat, tumbled out and, in moments, had fixed a hand firmly on Professor Wichmann's right elbow.

He looked round in sudden fright.

'It— It— But it's Detective Superintendent Martens.'

He had spoken with such unperturbed simplicity that she almost released her grip.

'But you—' she shot out. 'What are you doing here? You were—'

'Well, I have been taking a short holiday,' he replied quite cheerfully. 'However, just this morning, I realised that, for I believe the first time ever, I had left home without telling my good friend, Mr Chaudhuri, where I was going. So I decided I had better come back.'

Then he chuckled, china-white tombstone teeth glinting.

Harriet at last let go of his arm.

'Perhaps it is a good thing I came back,' he said. 'Because, you see, I did not go where I was going.'

'I'm sorry?'

'You do not understand? I can well believe that. Let me tell you what happened.'

And there and then on the wide pavement of University Boulevard he told his story.

'I had decided, as I said, to take a little walking holiday. To be plain, it was in part because of yourself. You remember I told you about my early days in Germany, and of how the threat of the Gestapo… But, never mind that. It was all long, long ago. But it has left me even now, I am sorry to say, with a fixed distrust of the police. Of any police. Even of you, my dear lady. So I thought I would go for a few days to walk in my favourite place, the Lake District.'

'Yes,' Harriet could not stop herself breaking in. 'I was right, you left your house at just the time to catch that train that ends up at Windermere.'

'So I did. So I intended to do, my dear Superintendent. I see you gave my affairs some most scholarly thought. If I left my flat at precisely nine-fifteen, you must have calculated, I could walk to the station in time for that train. But what you could not have known was that as I was walking along University Boulevard one of those sudden showers began, the ones that can become so heavy. And just then I saw a bus coming to a halt at the stop on the other side of the road. So I quickly crossed and jumped on it.'

A little toss of the head at the memory of his fleet-footedness.

'But, sitting on the top deck, as I love to do,' he went on, 'watching the rain splashing down I found I was thinking about a time long ago when, walking with my father in the Schwartzwald one day, we were caught in an *Aprilwetter*, and while we were sheltering under a tree from that heavy rain my father repeated to me a poem by Goethe set in that very forest, *Der Erlkonig*. You know about that malevolent little fellow, the Erlkonig?'

'No,' Harriet admitted, wondering what the point of this long account would turn out to be.

'So you do not speak any German? If you did, you would be bound to know that famous poem.'

'No, I'm sorry, I don't.'

What on earth is he on about?

'Very good. I will try to give you a version in English. It may not be very fine poetry. But I would like you to know what was in my head that day. So, listen.'

A solemn, throat-clearing cough. Then, standing there in

the middle of the broad pavement with the stiff breeze tossing his halo of white hair, he proclaimed.

'Who rides so late through night and wind?
It is the father with his child.
He has the boy well in his arms.
He grips him that way, he holds him warm.
My son, what makes you look so scared?
Do not you see, Father, the Erlkonig?
The Erlkonig with crown and—'

Professor Wichmann, arms wide in full flow, came to a halt.

'No, no, dear lady. This is not at all good. In English it would need many changes to have its true effect. Perhaps I should have made *Erlkonig* into Elf King. Yes. So now I will just go on to the finish. You see, the father promises his son all kinds of nice things at the journey's end. But the boy says... Yes, this is it:

My father, my father, now he has me fast,
The Elf King has me in the mournful land.
The father shudders, on he rides.
He holds in his arms the eight-year-old.
He reaches the Court in pain and distress.
In his arms the child is dead.'

There were tears in the old man's eyes now. Tears, and something more. Fear? Was it long-remembered fear? And why not? There was certainly something of dark menace in that poem he had heard as a child, clumsily though it had been told now.

'When that *Aprilwetter* there in the Schwartzwald was over,' Professor Wichmann went on, 'I wanted to take *Vati* by the hand. But he would not let me. You must learn to be brave, he told me.'

Harriet saw then that the old man had recalled that Black Forest walk so vividly that he was still actually trembling with fear, the fear, as he stood there now on the everyday pavement, of being snatched away by the Erlkonig, the Elf

King.

And suddenly she realised who the Elf King was for this eighty-year-old man. It was Detective Superintendent Harriet Martens, the threatening.

Should I...? Can I...?

But in a moment Professor Wichmann gave another little chuckle, and returned to his account of the day he had fled from Birchester.

'When that bus arrived at its destination, you see, the shower had not altogether come to an end. So I sat there on the top deck, all alone, reciting to myself Goethe's poem, more than once. And remembering. Then I found— Well, I found I had missed my train.'

Harriet laughed.

'But I think I know what you did then,' she said. 'You took the next train going to a place where you could go walking. You took the train that went right the way down to Brighton.'

'Yes, and I had some splendid days on the wonderful Sussex Downs. Until I remembered I had not mentioned to Mr Chaudhuri that I was going away.'

Should I tell him, Harriet asked herself. Should I tell him that even at this moment he is being hunted high and low across the hills of the Lake District? No. No, I won't. Why revive, even more acutely than my visits to him did, all his implanted fears of being suddenly arrested for no reason that he knows of?

She drove him then the short distance back to Bulstrode Road, and left him explaining to Mr Chaudhuri what had happened, at even greater length than he had explained it to her and with even more chuckling delight.

Turning at last in the right direction for home after giving Mr Brown the news about Professor Wichmann, she became abruptly conscious of that little irritating lost thought that had come to her, like a shred of something between two teeth. But when?

The time it had done so was at least easier to remember

than what it had been that had put that annoying little shred between her teeth. Yes, the time had been just after she had told John about her maddening visit to Aunty Beryl.

Ah, well, she thought, if he's at home for lunch, I can ask him about her as soon as I get in. And that may well bring back what it is that's been worrying me in this way.

John was at home. But what he immediately said as she came through the door, put all lesser concerns out of her head.

'Darling, I'm glad you're back. Listen, I was going to take the afternoon off. Crisis at Majestic resolved, thank goodness. A good deal of awkward negotiating by arch-negotiator John Piddock. So I thought why not go down to London and see Malcolm? You know my theory, *when there's nothing to be done, do nothing*. Well, there is nothing to be done for Malcolm at the moment; I phoned and asked. But all the same I thought I wouldn't for once, I'd do something. I'd buzz off down there and see him.'

He gave her a slightly shamefaced grin.

'But now you're here... You haven't got to go gadding off again, have you?'

'No. No, there's, if you like, *nothing to be done* by me here. So I can do something, with you. And we ought to go to Malcolm. He may be lying there, brooding and brooding over Graham. We ought to go. At once.'

'Well, I think a bite of lunch would be in order before we actually set off. I bought a sort of quiche thing on my way from the office, if that'll do. There'll be enough for two.'

The sort of quiche thing rapidly disposed of, they were in John's car barely half an hour later.

But now, as she sat there beside him, what nagged at her was the notion that there had been something she had wanted to ask John, something she could not in the least remember.

Then, as they entered the ward at St Mary's all thoughts of everything else vanished as if they had been just something skimmed over in a newspaper, thoughts of

Aunty Beryl – Yes, something to do with her fantasies of persecution – of Professor Wichmann, not after all fleeing from justice, of WAGI and her defeat there.

Malcolm was not sitting up absorbed in his Dick Francis nor looking at the endless parade of trivia on the TV screen on the wall opposite. He was lying flat on his back and his face seemed as pale as it had been when they had peered at him through the glass of the intensive care ward.

A relapse, she thought. Or... Or, worse, is it what bloody Beryl taunted me with? Has he fallen victim to MRSA, that bug – she was right – that doesn't yield to any antibiotic?

She looked up and down the ward for a nurse to ask.

And found that John – when there's something to be done, do it – had already slipped away and found someone in the glassed-off section at the far end.

Trying not to run, she joined him.

'No,' the nurse was saying, 'he's just suffering from temporary exhaustion. You know, when anyone's been as badly injured as he was, they're bound to have bad days as well as better ones.'

'Yes,' John said, 'I'd told myself that might be all that was the matter. But you know how it is, a parent's anxiety.'

So, back they went to Malcolm's bed, and hardly had they fetched chairs and sat quietly beside him than his eyes flickered open and a twitch of a smile appeared on his lips. But that was all he was able to manage and, after staying there for twenty minutes or so, by mutual consent they left.

It was as they were passing through the reception area that the sight of the burly security man there sent suddenly through Harriet's head a lightning trail of reasoning, or instinctive logic. It began with a recollection of the security men at Heronsgate House. Click, click, click, what they had said to her, how they had looked, became present in her mind. She saw the two of them, the big-boned Irishman and his heavy-built, indolent-looking partner, approaching from round the corner of the house. The quick looks they had exchanged when she had introduced herself as from the

police came up on her inner screen. Then the odd
reluctance of Winston Something – Yes, Earl – to show the
bruise on his face flicked up. Next she heard the Irishman,
O'Dowd, say how nearly he had become 'a burnt corpse'.
Then Winston's sheepishness about his overnight hospital
visit. Or had that been about the way he had tamely handed
over his keys? But no doubt about O'Dowd's pushful
insistence that his coat should be sniffed at for the petrol
smell remaining on it.

Don't all those things say something to me? Something
perhaps that, still suffering as I was that morning from the
immediate shock of Graham's death, I brushed aside, out of
a sort of fellow feeling for those two apparently shocked
Birchester Watchmen.

But *apparently* is surely the word.

Wasn't the whole pattern of their behaviour as
exaggerated as Aunty Beryl's was when I went to see her?
With her wild fear of drunks in the street, of violence, of
stalkers and, of all things, rape?

So, yes, that's why I kept being nagged at by that
irritating shred of thought between the teeth, there but
seemingly impossible properly to locate. This was it.

But, think now. Why were those two putting on that act?
In plain words, lying to me from start to finish?

All right, I'm going to find out.

Chapter Fourteen

Harriet, being driven home by John, sat going over in her mind the whole train of thought that had come to her at the sight of the security man at St Mary's. When she was sure the pattern she had seen was no wavering will-o'-the-wisp darting over the wide marshes of her ignorance about what had gone on when the CA 534 was stolen, she spoke.

'John, could you go by St Oswald's when we get into Birchester?'

'You feeling OK?'

She laughed.

'I'm fine. Sorry, I ought to have explained first, except I was deeply caught up in something that had just come to me.'

'Something not unconnected with the break-in at Heronsgate House?'

'All right, yes, you can read my mind. But one of the Birchester Watchmen there told me he'd had to go to St Ozzie's that night to have a wound to his head examined.'

'Oh, yes? And am I to be told why it was, as you sat deeply lost in thought, you suddenly decided you, too, had to go to St Ozzies tonight? Or is all this some keep-a-secret police work on behalf of your Mr Brown?'

'Well, yes, it is. I suppose it is.'

'So you just want me to take you to St Oswald's in pursuit of, as they say, your inquiries? And what then? Do I come and fetch you later on? Or do I urgently call Mr Brown if you're not back within an hour? Or should I just wait outside for a few minutes?'

'Probably that, if it's OK with you.'

'All right. So long as I get a bit of dinner some time tonight.'

'I promise.'

In the event John had to wait for less than ten minutes. In the hospital, Harriet found at the reception desk, late in the day though it was, a bright, young, absurdly blonde girl, spangly glitter at her ear lobes, who, as soon as a warrant card had been laid in front of and a question asked, opened her register and flipped back and forwards through its pages.

Eventually a little frown appeared between the spangly ear-rings.

'There isn't any entry for anyone coming in at that time on Tuesday night, or in the early hours of Wednesday. What did you say the name was again?'

'Earl, Winston Earl.'

'No, I'm certain. I've even checked the past three Tuesdays and Wednesdays, and no Winston Earl.'

'Thank you. That's all I wanted to know.'

Heading back to the car and vowing she would never again equate blondes with air-heads, Harriet felt a glow of satisfaction. Yes, there had been something fishy, very fishy, about the way the two of them, there outside the house, had tried to convince me they had done something which they had not.

The picture they had painted had been wrong. The one checkable fact in the whole rigmarole had made that crystal clear. Winston Earl had not needed hospital treatment for that bruise on the side of his face. He had not, as he had claimed, giving his blarneying mate a quick look of complicity, been so seriously hurt that he had had to go to St Oswald's.

But why exactly had the pair of them needed to pretend he had been hurt that badly?

I'm going to have a little chat with Winston Earl.

As soon as, at home, they had eaten their straight-from-the-freezer into the microwave supper, she went to the phone and called the Birchester Watchmen office.

But, bad news.

'Oh, yeah,' the night-shift girl who answered said. 'Yeah, we got a Winston Earl. Winny, nice bloke.'

'I asked where I could find him now.'

'I could look up in the book,' came the doubtful answer.

If this girl's a blonde, I go back on all I thought about them at St Ozzies.

'Then please do that.'

'Oh, OK. I suppose.'

'I told you this was a police inquiry.'

'Yeah, well, I suppose that's all right then.'

A long silence.

Harriet thought, once or twice, that she could hear pages of 'the book' being turned. She sat there sighing.

Then at last came the answer.

'Yeah. Yeah, I found it. Yeah, Winny's out at what they call South Birchester University. Used to be the Tech, you know. My Dad went there. I think.'

'You're sure? You're sure Winston Earl is on duty tonight at South Birchester University?'

'What it says in the book.'

'All right. Thank you. No. No, wait. Do you have a home address for him?'

'For my Dad?'

Harriet bit back an explosive retort.

'No. No, for Winston Earl.'

'Oh, yes. I know that. I been to it.'

'And it is...?'

'Oh, you want to know? Well, it's over in Moorfields. Just behind that pub, the Virgin an' Vicar, went to that with Winston once. Dead sexy.'

'The address?'

'Oh, yes. Yeah, it's Redwood Street. Number Fourteen.'

At last.

But under next morning's steady rain 14 Redwood Street proved not to be the single house the idiot girl at the Birchester Watchmen had implied. It was a tall, boot-faced anonymous block of flats, small windows going up and up in blank rows.

Yes, if she was a blonde, definitely an air-head one.

But I must see Winston Earl. Must, if need be, wake him

up from his sleep after night duty at South Birchester University, guarding all the expensive computers and machinery at the former tech.

Ah, a bit of luck. There just visible on the other side of these smeary glass entrance doors, underneath an intercom grille, a long row of bell-buttons, names beside them, however much surrounded by scrawled graffiti of every sort, phone numbers, rude drawings, invitations to *Come up for a Good Time.*

She pushed open the doors and went in.

Scan down the list. And... Yes, *Winston Earl 12B.* Finger pressed long and hard on the button.

And, more quickly than she expected, a good deal more quickly, a voice coming through the intercom grille.

'Yeah. Who that?'

She had no intention of identifying herself.

'Mr Earl, Winston Earl?'

'Thass me. What yer want?'

'I'd like a word. Can I come up?'

'A word? What about?'

'A matter of business, Mr Earl.'

'Business. I ain't got no business.'

'No, I realise that Mr Earl, but I would like to speak to you about some business I have.'

Is he being a bit too wary? Am I right? Has he recognised my voice? Better keep that lift there in sight, and the stairs, or I'll find he's off and away. And... And doesn't he sound somehow different from the man I remember from that conversation outside Heronsgate House? Maybe he's just got out of bed to answer the buzzer. Throat full of phlegm. Or maybe not.

And now no voice coming from the flat above.

'Mr Earl?'

'What you want?'

Oh, back to the beginning. What does he think he's going to gain this way?

All right, have to risk saying straight out who I am.

'Mr Earl, this is Detective Superintendent Martens. We spoke at Heronsgate House on Thursday morning. I have one or two things I'd like to ask you about.'

'Heronsgate House,' came the thickly voiced reply.

Then silence.

Then something more.

'Hey, man, you must be wanting Winston.'

'Yes. Yes, I am. Winston Earl.'

'No, you be wanting my son Winston. I'm Winston Earl. So's he.'

Dear God, I should have remembered. West Indian families often pass down forename along with surname.

'Yes, yes, Mr Earl, it's your son I want to speak to, the one who works for Birchester Watchmen.'

'He sleeping.'

'Then will you wake him? I'm coming up.'

Harriet found Winston Earl, the younger, in the bedroom which, to judge by the two single beds that took up most of its space, he must share with his wife-less father. The frowsty atmosphere, almost making her clamp her mouth shut, confirmed that the Birchester Watchmen guard had, until a few moments before, been sleeping off his night awake.

Then, her suspicions of Winston and his mate made her think, wryly, that Winston had probably spent at least a part of last night with his eyes comfortably shut. The glimpse she had had the morning after the break-in of the tossed-about duvet and head-dented pillow in the Director's bedroom came bouncing back into her mind.

When the bell at Heronsgate House had rung some time before midnight on Tuesday, no doubt the two Birchester Watchmen had been happily asleep on the Director's wide bed, head to tail. Didn't I, come to think, see a pillow at the bed's foot?

So, when she faced the young Winston Earl, slumped in stained T-shirt and creased boxer shorts on the edge of the bed in front of her, she challenged him with more than a little contempt.

'How's that bruise on your head today? Better than when you had to go to St Ozzies for it?'

Winston Earl blinked.

'Well?'

''s, OK, I guess.'

'Except that you never went near St Ozzies that night.'

Now the sleepy deep-brown eyes opened wide, with a look of something like plain fear.

'I— I did. I...'

'Don't try and lie your way out of it now. You've got a lot of explaining to do, Winston Earl. And, let me tell you, your only way to avoid finding yourself charged with obstructing police inquiries is to tell the whole truth now. From start to finish.'

Head hanging down, eyes fixed on the blackened toenails of his feet below. Silence.

'All right. Suppose you just answer the questions I put to you.'

A muttered 'OK.'

'First, where exactly were you when you were disturbed by the sound of the front-door bell?'

'I was— Well, sort of on the bed there.'

'Where? What bed?'

'Director's. We both of us were there. Big bed he got. An' soft.'

'All right. And, when you realised what bell it was you'd heard, you went tumbling down the stairs and opened that door without thinking. That it?'

'Yeah. Yeah, sort of.'

'And then what? Be careful how you answer.'

He took his time then. She could see the slow processes of his thoughts moving across his big, round, still sleep-sodden face.

'They stuck a gun in me belly. They did do that.'

'Oh, yes? But who was it who pushed that gun at you?'

Crunch question. At last a description, a true

description? Or just another fairy tale?

'Woman.'

'A woman? For God's sake...'

But, yes, she thought, if he's telling the truth, it could be... Damn it, it could be someone from WAGI.

Except that all the top-ranking WAGI members whom Gwendoline Tritton could trust to carry out the raid – and she would have to trust them indeed – were safely at that Council meeting, miles away at The Willows.

And then she realised that burly Winston was weeping, weeping from shame. Slow tears were wetting the stubbly flesh of his cheeks.

'Tell me all about it,' she said encouragingly.

'Yeah,' he managed to get out after half a minute or so. 'Yeah, they was women. They put it over on us, Mike an' me. Three bloody women. Just with that one gun.'

'They threatened to shoot one or the other of you? Unless you gave them your emergency key to the Director's office, that it? No petrol dousing, nothing of that sort? I suppose your fly Irish friend splashed some he found somewhere on himself after he'd concocted your story.'

'Yeah. It was Mike. Said we had to make something up or we'd be sacked, the both of us. So we— We sorta pretended we'd gone to St Ozzies.'

Tears still welling from his eyes.

Not the toughest of security guards, Harriet allowed herself to think. But what could you expect from cheapo Birchester Watchmen? And, if by some chance I'm right about WAGI and, after all, Maggie Quirke did learn from Christopher about the CA 534 and where it was hidden, then mightn't she have gathered from him at some other time what inefficient people were guarding Heronsgate House.

Any more to learn from this poor blubbering fellow on the bed?

'So what happened after you'd given that key to one of

those women?'

'Other two tied us up, didn't they? They had that gun. What could we do? Had to let 'em.'

'And some time after they'd all gone— Did you see if the one who went up to the Director's office was carrying anything when she came back?'

'Couldn't, could I? Made us lie down, face to the wall.'

He looked up now, wiping a hand across his tear-blotched face.

'Weren't no good at tying, though, they weren't. Got loose ten minutes after they ran off.'

A miniscule burst of pride.

Harriet left him, consoling himself with that.

Chapter Fifteen

Sitting in the shelter of her car outside the boot-faced Moorfields block of flats, Harriet thought over the situation that blubbery Winston's confession had brought to light. So, the midnight raid at Heronsgate House had been the work, not of heavies invented by Michael O'Dowd, but of a handful of women. Three vigorous and determined women who knew just what they were looking for, and just where to find it.

So how did they come to have that knowledge? Answer, almost certainly, through Christopher Alexander. He told me in that confused phone call of his that he'd *let slip*, as he defended himself on the mattress he shared with taunting Maggie Quirke, fully-fledged member of the Council of Women Against Genetic Interference, both the fact that Dr Lennox had kept a sample of CA 534 and where it was that he had concealed it.

And what organisation was more likely to have sent that ultimatum letter declaring that unless research into *genetically modified foods* was brought to an immediate end a highly destructive herbicide would be let loose? All right, in theory that could be half a dozen other militant groups. But how would any of them, even if they had the will to issue a threat like that, have got hold of that information about CA 534?

So doesn't it come down now to surrounding the solidly respectable The Willows? To searching the whole place from top to bottom until that appallingly destructive substance is found?

But, as soon as she had formulated that question, a sharp doubt came into her mind. A surfacing submarine, ready with threatening torpedoes.

Oh, yes, on the face of it I have worked my way to the solution. Except that it doesn't square with one very awkward fact. Fifteen of Gwendoline Tritton's most active subordinates were at a Council meeting at The Willows, miles away from Heronsgate House, at the time of the break-in. A fact, curiously, made firmer because there were not, at midnight, sixteen members at the meeting. Aunty Beryl's departure at 8.06 p.m. had been carefully recorded in the sacrosanct Minutes Book.

All right, when the hunt switched so decisively to Professor Wichmann I didn't bother to check those fifteen Council members to see if, unlikely possibility that it was, that whole alibi had been cooked-up. True, Gwendoline Tritton, rigid believer that whatever she does is the best that can be done, would be well capable of dreaming up a large-scale alibi like that. But, when you look at it, such a scheme has to be leaky as an old bucket. Fifteen witnesses all lying, and lying successfully, each of them made word-perfect.

Will Mr Brown see a way out of that? I think perhaps I'll go and talk to him rather than using the mobile. This is going to need some prolonged consideration.

The ACC, when she gave him her account of what she had learnt from Winston Earl and the implications as she saw them, drew down his long upper lip in deep thought. Harriet had begun to wonder, once more, whether she was expected to put in a 'Sir?' or some other prompt. But at last he delivered his verdict.

'Yes.'

One decision-heavy syllable.

'Well now, Superintendent, despite what you say, about the Minutes of that Council meeting of theirs, I think the time has finally come for a full-scale search of Gwendoline Tritton's place. Provided always that your assessment of her is correct.'

'I think it is, sir. You've only to look at her. She really believes—' For a moment she scratched around for a convincing phrase, and found it. 'You may know, sir, a couplet of Pope's – my husband's always quoting it – that goes:

'Tis with our judgments as our watches, none
Go just alike, yet each believes his own.

Well, Gwendoline Tritton would believe her own watch,
even if it was two hours out.'

'Pope, did you say? Alexander Pope?'

A good Scots education.

'Yes, sir, Pope. And I think I haven't misquoted him.'

'Never mind if you have. You've made your point. A lady
who knows for certain that whatever she happens to think
is inevitably right. Yes, she might well believe she has some
sort of title to that CA 534.'

'I can go along with that, sir.'

'Very good. A raid will need some careful planning,
however. We must keep the number of officers concerned
to an absolute minimum. Until the CA 534 is safe in our
hands we must let as few people as possible know that for a
time it was not. But, if we're going to have to search that
house— What did you say it was called?'

'The Willows, sir.'

'Very good. If we put a search team into The Willows,
they'll have to know just what it is we expect them to find,
that wee cardboard box, or maybe just that thickened glass
tube, containing – didn't you say? – some millilitres of oily
yellow liquid. But, even if they find nothing, and they may
well do that, mind you, then before too long it'll be all
round the Police Club and all the police pubs that
something secret has been stolen from Heronsgate House,
and then the whole sorry tale will come out. Come out in
the press, as likely as not, with people like that young man
from the *Star* hanging round offering drinks. And you
know what a story in one of the papers will mean. There'd
be another wild panic to add to those al-Qaeda is creating
with their discovery that no more than a simple threat can
cause the wicked West almost as much damage as 9/11 did.'

He looked at Harriet across the surface of his austere,
almost paperless desk.

'So can I entrust you with finding the minimum team

necessary, officers of proven reliability?'

'Yes, sir.'

'When you've done that we'll choose a time. But don't waste so much as a minute preparing. If you're right about that woman Tritton, she won't keep holding above us the threat of CA 534 much longer. She'll be using the stuff somewhere. If she's got it at all, of course.'

It took Harriet all that afternoon, working from home while John was down in London at the inquest on Graham – something he had forbidden her even to think of attending – to assemble the sort of team Mr Brown had in mind. Not all the officers she chose were top-ranking skilled searchers. But, as she had selected them from detectives, men and women, she had worked with at various times, she felt safe in believing they were possessed of skills enough to do the job. To them, however, she added two officers she did not know well, Detective Sergeant Jones and DC Emma Hardy, specialists from the Force Searches Team.

So, by the end of that day – each of her choices carefully interviewed – she felt, bar one other small task yet to be done, that she would be ready to go to Mr Brown the next morning to choose the moment to act.

The one other task she had set for herself was to go and have a careful look at The Willows from outside. If, when the search team presented themselves there, Gwendoline Tritton, small box tucked beneath that knobby-buttoned jacket, made her escape at the back, the whole enterprise would fall apart.

From the row of hooks by the garden door she took down an old mackintosh of John's, an ancient, seldom used garment, occasionally lent out to friends caught in the rain.

Mannish though it is, she thought as she set out into the fast-fading evening light, it'll serve as a reasonable disguise if ferocious Miss Tritton chances to be looking out. And it may always come on to rain again.

In the event, there was no sign of the house's owner

when Harriet went slowly walking past it along wide Pargeter Avenue. Between The Willows and its neighbours on either side, high brick walls still ensured respectable privacy in this fast-deteriorating area, the Meads. She walked on then to the next turning so as to inspect the house from the rear. Reaching the road there, one a good deal less well-kept than Pargeter Avenue, she set off again for the back of the big, old house, conscious of the creaking sound John's stiff mack was making at her every step.

All was tranquilly quiet, despite this plainly being a part of the area that had descended into social chaos. The cars left at the kerbsides looked even more on the edge of the scrap yard than those outside Christopher Alexander's flat. Few of the streetlights appeared to have come on, although it must be well into lighting-up time. On the opposite pavement, beside all the usual rubbish that collects in seldom-swept streets, there lay, she saw, a large branch ripped off a fully blossoming lilac in one of the patches of front garden, relic of distant, different days.

She looked at it for a moment, depressed at the senseless hooliganism it demonstrated. And then, as she had done often enough in the past, she told herself that the impulse to destroy was, after all, simply a sign that there were too many of the deprived, reduced to expressing their discontent in the only way they could see to do it. By destroying, or – what's the word? – besmirching what seemed like a threat to them from the well-regulated world.

She walked on, looking upwards into the clear sky for the line of ornate chimney stacks that marked out The Willows.

Then, as their shapes slowly made themselves clear, in the silence of the deserted street, somewhere ahead she heard clanking footsteps. In a moment she was able to make out, in the faint light from the single streetlamp she could see, the person coming towards her, a big swaggering black man, head crowned with a yellow woolly cap. And at once, totally irrationally, she felt a tingle of menace.

All right, she said to herself, I know plenty of black

villains, many of them almost as much pussycats as poor, blubbering Winston Earl. But I was brought up, down on the South Coast, among my parents' older friends, more or less relics of the Raj. And they instinctively feared and despised anyone with a dark skin. So, yes, if I'm not afraid, I am at least alert. The shadow of old, forgotten haunted feelings.

Or perhaps I'm resurrecting those because...because I want an excuse, the excuse that I've been somehow threatened, not to go on with this on my own. It's the climax, or it may be the climax. And, truth to tell, deep down I may really be afraid of the outcome. Of failure. Even of success, too. Success achieved through more violence than I can handle now. Yes, old though she is, Gwendoline Tritton, is liable to turn to violence – a knife from the kitchen, a four-pronged fork from the garden – violence that may bring about death. Another unnecessary death in a world too full of them.

She came to a halt. The high back wall of The Willows was too close to be able to spend time giving it the careful scrutiny needed before the big man approaching her came level.

In a minute now he was all but face-to-face with her. And she saw at once that, eyes fixed on the ill-swept pavement at his feet, he was in no way a threat to anybody.

No, poor devil, she thought as he swerved a little and passed her by, he's probably in the depths of depression. Perhaps – the idea struck her with sudden force – he, too, has just lost a loved one.

Graham, poor dead, blown to pieces Graham.

Behind her the clanking footsteps slowly receded. Above, in The Willows, a solitary light came on in one of the windows.

No, damn it, she told herself, I'm here to carry out a task. Come back, Hologram Harriet. Haul me out of this, make me get on with it.

And it happened. Whether she was the hologram or the

real Harriet, she went a few steps further until she found in the high wall a tall, narrow wrought-iron gate. Recently repainted, she noted. No lack of money here. She tried to rattle its bars. Solidly immovable.

Well and good. If when tomorrow we come knocking at Gwendoline Tritton's front door, she attempts to slink off this way with the CA 534, I'll have the heftiest officer in my team posted here to stop her. Oh, yes, better have a woman officer, too, it may come to a body search.

She took one last look at the looming shape of the big house. The one lit window in it was abruptly extinguished.

Good, now for a quiet night at home and in the morning a conference with Mr Brown.

At home, however, she was soon to find the best laid plans of mice and men – another favourite John quotation – do 'gang aft a-gley'. Hardly had she restored the stiff old mack safely to its accustomed peg than she heard John at the front door, and, his topcoat hardly off, asked him about the inquest, her head crowded once more with thoughts of Graham – her baby, the boy at school, the young man at college, the probationary police officer, the dead slumped body in Notting Hill's Ladbroke Walk.

'Oh well,' John answered her, 'you know how these things go, you ought to after all. A lot of dreary questions and very seldom any startling revelations. Some poor fellow from the police station had to give evidence about finding Graham. Pretty nasty for him. What was it he said? Yes, "whom I recognised from a part of the remains as my fellow officer, PC Graham Piddock". But I did manage afterwards to have a brief word with him, thank him. And the verdict, of course, was that usual formal *murder by a person or persons—*'

The phone rang then.

Harriet, the thought of that call from Superintendent Robertson bursting into her mind again, snatched it up. It was only out of well-drilled habit that she simply gave the number and no more.

But no one spoke in answer. Yet – she listened more intently – there seemed to be some faint background noise there.

Then she heard something else, something odd.

Yes. Yes, that's it. Someone's clinking something – a coin? – on some nearby window or other.

Wait. Yes. It's on the side of, surely, a phone-box.

So, what is this? I don't get many calls from a box nowadays. Not like in the old *Stop the Rot* time in B Division when I used quite often to get a threatening message from some no-good I was targeting.

'Hello,' she said, clearly, if a little cautiously. 'Who's calling?'

Still silence.

But, yes, the familiar heavy breathing of old. Though this hardly seems really heavy.

'Hello, can you hear me? Who do you want to speak to?'

Then a voice, on the edge of being recognisable. Female, croaking a little.

'Harriet?'

Now, who's this? Calling me Harriet, and, yes, it does seem to be somebody I know. But certainly not, from her voice, one of what John calls my *mates*.

'I've got something important to tell you. It's Beryl Farr, John's Aunt—'

The call at that moment clicked to an end. Blank silence.

'John, it was Aunty Beryl. I think in a phone-box. But it sounds as if she's been cut off.'

Aunty Beryl, silly old fool, she thought, must have put in just one single coin. Probably still believes it's enough for a long chat, may not have used a call-box for months, years even.

But what's she calling about? Asking not for John, but me. *Harriet*. And with, she said, something important to tell me. What? What could she have to tell me? Something that she, at least, thinks important? Yes, she must have had to come out to make her call in the dark, the dark she so dislikes.

So why then doesn't she fish out another coin and call again? Preferably pull out a whole purse-full.

For half a minute more, for a full minute, she stood waiting for the ringing sound. Then she told herself the truth. Aunty Beryl hasn't got any more coins. She went out to that call-box clutching just a single carefully selected one. And now she is standing there, feeling trumped by Fate.

But which call-box is she in? And will she stay there long enough for me to jump in the car, find her? No, Moorfields and her flat were too far away.

So... What?

Yes, this is it.

She looked round for her bag – there on the floor by her chair – grabbed it, snatched out her mobile, thumbed the number she miraculously recalled for British Telecom's local, police-linked number-chasing line.

'Good evening, Detective Superintendent Martens. Perhaps you remember me?'

'Oh, yes. Yes, Mrs Martens. It's Ireen. We've often chatted. What can I do for you?'

'I've just had a call, from— From one of my snitches, probably in a box somewhere in the Moorfields area. They got cut off, and don't seem to be trying to get through again. Can you do some urgent checking?'

'No trouble, Mrs Martens.'

'Good work. I'm on my mobile by the way. I'll give you the number.'

'OK. I'll call you back, soon as.'

Thank goodness for old contacts, and ones kept warm. And forgive me, Ireen, for lying to you about my *snitch*, bringing a little, hurry-up excitement into your life. But if Beryl isn't exactly a common-or-garden snitch, she is, or she may be, an informant.

But what about? What was she going to inform me of? And will Ireen be able to locate that call-box in time for me to ring her there? Or will she have left and gone back in the dark to her grim-looking lair? In the dark, where, John told me, she never ventures out.

Absolutely afraid to go out at night. Yes, that's precisely what John said. Not, as I thought there at The Willows when I was looking at that big Minutes Book again, disliking being out late at night. If Aunty Beryl never, really never, goes out at night, she won't at all have left that WAGI Council meeting as late as a few minutes past eight o'clock, fully dark then at this time of year. So ferocious Gwendoline Tritton must have had her name added to that list of *Those Present*, together with that somehow convincingly precise *Left meeting* at 8.06 p.m., just in order to make me think the midnight meeting did really take place, trusting I wouldn't believe it necessary actually to go to that grotty flat in Moorfields to check. Which, in fact, I did not do, even when I paid Beryl my visit.

She stood looking at the phone.

Ring, won't you, ring. Find one more coin at the bottom of your handbag, Aunty Beryl, fumble it into the slot. Obey the written instructions in front of you and call me.

Her mobile sprang to life. She grabbed it, gabbled out her number.

'It's Ireen, Mrs Martens. That call seems to have been made in a box at the corner of Harrington Street in Moorfields. Let me give you its number. I'd think that'd be your quickest way to get back to him.'

Him? Him? Who the hell— Oh, God, yes, my famous snitch. She's bound to have seen it as a man.

'Let's have it, Ireen. You're a miracle worker.'

In less than a minute she was dabbing out on her phone the call-box number. It rang. It rang and rang.

Aunty Beryl, are you there? Don't tell me you've gone back through the dark evening to your urine-smelly home.

The ringing stopped. A trembling voice said 'Yes?'

'Beryl? Beryl, it's me, Harriet.'

'Oh, good. You know, I didn't expect to be cut off so

quickly. Not when I'd put in as much as I had. I think that's extortionate. Someone ought to do something about it.'

'Yes. Yes, I agree. Absolutely. But you said you had something to tell me?'

'Did I? Oh, yes. Yes, of course I did. But, you know, there've been a lot of nasty little boys all round the kiosk here, shouting and tapping at the glass, and everything's gone right out of my head.'

Oh, God. No.

'Listen, Aunt— Listen, Beryl. Are the boys still there?'

'Well, no. No. They ran off in the end, when they saw I was just standing here.'

'All right, then. Now, can you think? You were going to tell me something you said was import—'

'Oh, yes. Yes, of course. The daffodils. It was so kind of you to bring me them. I put them in water straight away, and, do you know, they're as fresh today as when you gave them to me.'

Must go easy with her. Must.

'Well, I'm glad. I love daffodils at this time of year, a promise of all the good weather to come. But didn't you say what you had to tell me was important? Can you remember what it was?'

'Of course I can.' A touch of the old familiar scratchiness. 'I had a visit earlier today from Gwendoline Tritton. And she didn't bring me flowers, I can tell you that.'

'But why did she visit you? Does she often come?'

'Of course not. Too wrapped up in herself and her doings, Gwendoline. Always was. No, she came specially. And do you know what she wanted me to do?'

I think I do, Harriet said to herself. I think I do, and if I'm right it's exactly what I need to know.

'Yes, Beryl?'

'She told me she had put in the Minutes of the WAGI Council that I had been present on the night of Tuesday, March the sixteenth. But I wasn't present. And I told her so. She ought to have known I never set foot outside after dark. Never. She ought to have known that, but, as I say, too wrapped up in herself to think about anybody else.'

'Yes, I've met her, and I agree.'

'Well, do you know what she told me to do then? Ordered me to do? She told me that if anybody asked, and she mentioned you by name, Harriet, by name and police rank... She said I was to say I was there at that meeting. Well, I let her believe I would do it. There's no arguing with some people, you know.'

'Quite right. The only way to deal with someone like that.'

She thought furiously. Found no way of ending the call in any sort of a tactful manner.

'But— But I'm sorry, Beryl, I'll have to ring off now. Something very urgent's come up.'

And, yes, she thought, it was quite right of you, Aunty Beryl, to venture out in the dark to that call-box, once you couldn't smother your conscience a moment longer, to tell me what Gwendoline Tritton had demanded that you lie about.

'John,' she said. 'Listen, I think I may have to go out. Aunty Beryl's stuck at this time of night in a call-box in Moorfields. I'd better go— Or, no. No, I'll ring the local PS. That'd be quicker after all.'

She rang the Moorfields police station. And put down the phone, happy in the thought that a good solid PC would soon be on his way to escort Aunty Beryl back home.

Then, yes, she thought, I was right to tell the poor old thing that *something urgent* has come up. It's an urgent matter now to make the raid on The Willows, before Gwendoline Tritton perhaps condescends to think a little about her church-mouse friend of old and realises she may not have done what she was commanded to do.

'Listen,' she said to John, 'could you order a take-away supper? I've got work to do, calls to make.'

Chapter Sixteen

Once again the phone rang.

Aunty Beryl back? Something more about the daffodils? But, no. No, can't be her, she's right out of coins.

She picked up the handset, began reciting the number.

'Mum?'

The single syllable interrupting her struck like a hammer-blow.

What? What can— This can't be— It's an hallucination. I'm going mad—

'Mum, it's me. Malcolm. Are you there?'

'Malcolm, Malcolm. It's you.'

She could still hardly believe it was his voice in her ear. Somehow she had been thinking of him all along as infinitely removed from her own everyday life. As if, ill as he was, he was in a wholly different country. In Hospitalia.

And now he was here. Or on the other end of a simple telephone line. Part of life.

She felt her whole world, only days ago when she heard Superintendent Robertson ploddingly giving her the news that had seemed to turn everything in a moment upside down, now moving slowly towards where it ought to be. That great iron plate she had felt herself fixed to was slowly revolving back to the place it had been in when the world was altogether different, when Superintendent Robertson was not even a name to her. It was as if an iceberg, freed by global warming, was, against all expectations, drifting back towards the North Pole.

Malcolm. Malcolm, here at the end of the phone.

'Yes, of course it's me, Mum,' she heard him cheerfully go on. 'Who else did you think it could be?' A sudden halt. 'Oh. Oh, Jesus, yes, I shouldn't have said that. Shouldn't really have thought it. Who else could it be, if it wasn't me? Only Graham. Poor Graham. You never did learn to sort out our two voices, did you? Dad did. But it was always possible to trick you when we were kids. I'm sorry, Mum. I shouldn't have started on this without thinking. I should have picked my words better. Sorry.'

'No, it's all right, darling. I didn't really think it might be Graham. Or his ghost or something. No, I knew it was you, but it came as such a surprise. Where are you phoning from? Your bed? Have they brought you one of those trolleys?'

'Yes. Yes, that's it. They asked me, now they're able to hoist me up into some sort of sitting position, if I'd like to call home. But, Mum, I've got some even better news.'

'Yes? Yes, darling?'

'The great Sir Thing, on his round this morning, told me: guess what.'

'No, you tell me.'

'He said he thought it was OK now for them to operate on my worst leg. One of those bits of metal cut right through the tendon that's meant to keep the knee-cap where it should be. So now it's going to be hooked into place again. They didn't like to do it till I was fit enough to have the anaesthetic. It's only a minor op, actually. That's if you can believe old Sir. You know what those Lords of Creation are like.'

'Oh, Malcolm, that's marvellous. Marvellous. I thought— We thought you might never be able to walk again. But— But this means that you will be? Doesn't it? Does it?'

'Well, yes, it looks like that. It's what Sir Thing— I've never been able to twist round enough to see his painted name hanging there over my head after that first time. But he said it is on the cards. That eventually I'll be walking.'

After news like that there seemed to be little more worth saying. She managed, chatting on for a little and longing to hand over to John, not to talk about the future. The thought of what might go wrong over the operation, minor or not, had begun to loom too heavily. And thoughts of MRSA, scourge of all hospitals, threatened by poor Aunty

Beryl, heroic darkness-defying Aunty Beryl, there in her poky flat, not really very urine-smelling.

So, as soon as Malcolm had come to a breathless halt – 'got to pay for this eventually, you know, costing a fortune' – she handed the phone to John.

And then she had made her call from her mobile to Mr Brown to tell him what she had just learnt about commanding Gwendoline Tritton.

'Very good,' he answered. 'That settles it. It's the final piece of evidence we need. That attempt to establish a multiple person alibi – extraordinary thing to do – is just blown away. Good work, Harriet. I'll get hold of my tame magistrate and ask for a search warrant for tomorrow. I'd prefer to go in there by daylight, too many chances for things to go wrong in the dark. So can you have your team ready for, say, 8 a.m?'

'Yes, sir. No trouble. They're all on alert.'

'Very good. I'll get the warrant sent round to you straight away.'

Harriet, down in Moorfields, tasked her team at 7.30, only just fully light, still cold, but no rain. Vehicles, when they moved off, to be kept well out of sight round the corner from The Willows. The two officers to wait in the back road, in case Miss Tritton did attempt to make a break for it. Task allocated to Searches Team members, DS Jones and DC Emma Hardy, used to working together. Once Tritton had been secured indoors, they could be let in to supervise.

By 07:55 everyone had moved into place, looking in their anti-contamination overalls like creatures from a TV programme for tiny tots. Harriet alone was in uniform. If Gwendoline Tritton was to be impressed with the seriousness of the raid, anything to overawe her was worth doing. The search warrant tucked into her top pocket was all too likely, she thought, to be scorned as a piece of police scheming to frustrate the perfectly proper aims of WAGI.

Harriet, eyes on her watch, at last gave the signal and led the bulk of her team along towards the wide Pargeter

Avenue ahead.

Then, as she heard the sound of a noisy vehicle starting up just beyond, she brought them to a halt, her arms held wide to either side.

'Hang on a sec.'

She crouched well down at the corner of the high wall of the house at the road's end and peered round. A small car, issuing a great cloud of exhaust fumes, was just buzzing away in the opposite direction.

'All clear. OK, let's go.'

They ran forwards now. 08:00 hours precisely.

With a pulsing feeling of success just ahead, Harriet mounted the steps to the broad front door of The Willows and viciously thumbed the fat button of the bell.

Almost immediately the door was swept open wide, and Gwendoline Tritton stood there. A familiar figure, still in the long wool skirt in bold patches of orange and yellow, the dull green jacket buttoned all the way up, the planked-down faded blue trainers.

But her arms were complacently folded across her scrawny chest and on her bony face, behind the huge spectacles, there was, unmistakably, the look of triumph.

Triumph. Why?

Then in Harriet's head there bloomed, like a swift-unfolding Japanese water flower dropped into a tall glass, an ugly piece of knowledge. The car she had just seen buzzing away along the wide road outside had been painted in bright psychedelic colours. And she had last seen such a vehicle parked outside Christopher Alexander's flat. And who was Christopher's girlfriend but Maggie Quirke? Member of Gwendoline Tritton's selected Council, and young and athletic.

She jumped down the steps from that big front door, tugging out her mobile as she landed.

Jab, jab, jab at the buttons for Mr Brown's number.

'Superintendent Martens, sir. Can you get a stop radio-call out to halt a car, a Mini painted in psychedelic colours, green, purple and more. Don't know the number. It's probably being driven by one Maggie Quirke. Seen barely two minutes ago, heading along Pargeter Avenue in a – let me see – yes, westerly direction.'

'Pargeter Avenue, westwards. Very well.'

Five sharp, Scots-accented words, and no more.

Harriet climbed, a little leadenly, up the steps to The Willows door again. She took the search warrant from the pocket of her uniform and rang once more at the fat button of the bell. A long-held summons.

All right, it's almost certain that the CA 534 is no longer inside this monster of a house. It's been whisked away from under our noses by Maggie Quirke. But if Gwendoline Tritton thinks she's put one over on Greater Birchester Police, then she's going to learn that we don't take that sort of trickery lightly. We're going to turn this place over from cellars to attics, and leave her to clear up the mess.

And then she asked herself how it could have come about that Miss Tritton had some idea, or premonition, that The Willows was about to be raided and had no doubt summoned Maggie Quirke at some late hour of the night.

At once the likely answer arrived.

That light I saw in the window at the back of the house last night. Miss Tritton, perhaps wandering anxiously about her big empty house, must have heard the same clanking footsteps out at the back as I did, that big, distressed-looking man. And she had flicked on a light and looked out. And just then had seen something. My outline against the narrow gate as I tried it? But that could have been enough.

There was a longer wait now for the front door to be opened, but eventually it was drawn back, though not very far.

Harriet thrust her search warrant in at the gap, careful to keep a tight grip on it.

'A search warrant?' Miss Tritton said, pulling the door a little wider open. 'Very well, conduct your search, though I hardly think you'll find whatever it is you're looking for.'

Stony-faced, Harriet pushed her way past her.

'Bill,' she said to the DC she had plucked from her old haunt in B Division, 'ask this lady for the key to the back gate here and let the Searches Team people in would you?'

She saw Miss Tritton deciding whether to make difficulties over the key or not, and thinking in the end that things were going so much her way that any more obstruction would be over-egging the pudding.

She set her searchers methodically to work then, starting from the two cellars, the coal and the wine, both nowadays empty and echoing.

As soon as she could she hunted out Gwendoline Tritton again. A lady more than capable, she thought, if the CA 534 box had not after all been given to Maggie Quirke, of surreptitiously removing it from some hiding place above and replanting it somewhere where she knew the searchers had completed their work. She found her in the big drawing room, now the office of WAGI. She was sitting on a chair from the dining room next door, bolt upright, staring straight ahead through the heavy-rimmed spectacles on her bony nose, that smile of triumph lingering on her face. She did not deign to give even a nod of greeting.

Expecting to be in the place for hours to come, Harriet sought out another chair and sat down. But in a few minutes her mobile warbled.

'Yes?'

It was Mr Brown.

'Some good news, I think. A squad car has picked up your psychedelic Mini with the young lady, Maggie Quirke, in it. She's stopped for petrol at a service station at the city end of University Boulevard. I imagine she was making for the motorway to tuck herself into hiding somewhere in London. Now, the place can't be all that far from the Meads, so I suggest you go along and assist.'

'Right. Petrol station at this end of University Boulevard. I'll be there in ten minutes.'

At the petrol station Harriet found a police vehicle neatly slewed across its exit and two uniformed officers standing looking, po-faced, at the young woman who must be the driver of the psychedelic Mini beside the pumps, Maggie Quirke.

She got out of her car, with DC Emma Hardy whom she had thought worth bringing with her, and walked over.

'Good morning, Miss Quirke.'

No answer.

'I am Detective Superintendent Martens, Greater Birchester Police, and this is Detective Constable Hardy. I have reason to believe you may have in your car or on your person a small cardboard box containing a single test tube filled with an oily yellow liquid.'

'Oh, have you?'

A jaunty look.

Poor pretty-faced Christopher, she thought, he must have caught himself a tiger by the tail here. Unless, of course, she was the one who had decided, dedicated WAGI member as she is, to catch him.

'Do I take it you deny you are in possession of that test tube?'

'Of course I do.'

Harriet permitted herself a little smile.

'I notice,' she said, 'you don't ask what that oil is and why we are anxious to retrieve it.'

'What if I don't?'

'Just that this indicates to me that you do have it and that you know very well what the liquid it contains is.'

'Find it then.'

'Very well. First DC Hardy will search you personally, and I should warn you that it will, if necessary, be an intimate procedure.'

A quick glance to see if the implicit threat had produced

any reaction.

None.

'So, come inside, and I'll ask the people here if there's an office or a room somewhere that we can make use of.'

She looked back to where the two PCs were waiting beside their vehicle.

'I think you'd better hang on here,' she called out. 'I may have someone for you to take in before much longer.'

She ushered Maggie into the building then. And, yes, the attendant in charge was only too happy to help the police.

'Got a lot o' time for the boys in blue. And the girls. You do a night shift here, and you'll be all the happier to think they come calling every now and again.'

'I'm glad we're in your good books.'

So the little office at the back, its grimy white-washed walls decorated with nudie calendars going back half-a-dozen years, was cleared of the few things the attendant might need and handed over.

Harriet looked round.

'Just pull that blind down over the window,' she said to DC Hardy. 'And I'll ask to have any customers kept out of the way for the next few minutes.'

A glance at Maggie to see if the promised search of her person had now brought any signs of anxiety. Nil result.

Propping herself against the till then, Harriet watched Emma Hardy put down her heavy black case of search tools on the deeply grease-spotted table in the corner, take from it a pair of dull white surgical gloves and ease each one over her hands.

Still no reaction from Maggie.

Then, first, she was carefully frisked. Next she was asked to remove, piece by piece, each item of her clothes, and Emma's firm gloved fingers probed every conceivable hiding-place in them. At last came the body search itself, with Emma from time to time giving her subject quiet instructions.

Harriet patted herself on the back now for having,

despite some misgivings over the security aspect, taken on
her two highly trained Searches Team officers. If the CA
534 was on, or in, Maggie Quirke's person, it was going to
be found. Perhaps at any moment. And if that small
reinforced test tube was hidden somewhere among
Maggie's possessions or elsewhere in her psychedelic little
car, then it was going to be brought to light.

Or, even if, after all, it's still somewhere inside The
Willows, she thought, DS Jones will lay his hands on it,
however tricksy Gwendoline Tritton's been in concealing it.

Eventually, it seemed that Maggie did not have the tube
on her.

Looking at her as she sulkily put her clothes back on,
Harriet decided it might be no bad thing to upset her a little
more.

'So you were on your way to London?' she said.

The casual inquiry did produce, as it was meant to, a
flicker of anxious response.

Aha, good sign. We're definitely on the right track. That
box will be somewhere in her car, almost bound to be.

'Yes, I was going to London. Why shouldn't I? I've
turned in my job, so I'm a free agent.'

'You were on the *Chronicle*, weren't you? I wonder why
you left. Perhaps they'll tell me there.'

Show her we know a lot about her and can find out still
more. A bit of un-nerving will do no harm.

Yes. Seems my little threat's done its work. Those
gleaming white teeth Tim Patterson went on about have
momentarily clamped themselves together.

But she got no more than that one hint of anxiety.

So Emma Hardy's search moved on to the car in the
forecourt. One by one she brought in from it Maggie's
luggage and the other miscellaneous objects that
accumulate in a car. She stacked them neatly underneath the
rickety-looking, oil-stained table ready to be dealt with.

But when the pile was complete it took much longer than
Harriet had hoped to go through it, item by item. Maggie

Quirke sat there on an aged typist's chair and watched as Emma's neatly moving fingers turned each case, each bulging plastic supermarket bag, inside-out. And gradually a smirk of a smile glinted out from those white teeth. At last it had to be acknowledged that all Emma's efforts so far had come to nothing. Soon only the psychedelic Mini itself would be left.

Harriet, having watched Emma at work, had no doubts she would be perfectly capable of taking the little car completely to bits if that had to be done. But after almost an hour, with only two or three items of the car clutter remaining, she could keep her patience no longer.

'Let me deal with a few of these things,' she said to the probing DC, bent low over the grease-engrained table.

She got a quick assessing look, junior officer to high-up.

'I think I'd better tackle them myself, ma'am,' the reply came then. 'You really need to be specially trained for this sort of work.'

Harriet produced a smile of understanding.

'I dare say you're right. But should I phone for more help? No doubt DS Jones could be spared from The Willows now.'

'As you think fit, ma'am. But often one pair of hands is better than two. Nothing gets missed in error that way. But, if you like, I could go and tackle the car itself. The little that's left here isn't actually very likely to yield any treasure.'

'All right, why don't you go out and do that? And let's hope you find yourself getting lucky at last.'

A pleasure really, Harriet thought, watching her through the office's smeary window as she stood assessing the old Mini, to see someone so confidently at work at a task they know down to its last detail.

She turned then and gave a quick glance at the girl perched on the battered typist's chair. But, it appeared, that moment of thought looking out of the window, had lost her the chance of seeing whether her reference to 'getting lucky' had produced a reaction. Maggie still had lurking on her lips that smirk of a smile.

Am I wrong, Harriet thought, with a sudden descent from optimism. Have I been wrong all along? Has Gwendoline Tritton never had the CA 534? Was the raid on Heronsgate House organised by some other outfit altogether?

She sat there leaning against the till, battling this onset of drained-away confidence. And before long found herself immersed in that other, and deeper, source of misery.

Graham, Graham, Graham, her mind kept grindingly repeating. Graham, my son, my son in his prime, is dead. Killed. Killed. Killed.

What does all this search nonsense matter set against that one brutal stone block of fact. Graham is dead, dead before his time.

Her ever-descending maelstrom of misery and grief was ended by a sudden interruption. She had heard a car drawing up outside, but in her absorption had taken no particular notice. During the time they had been in the little office several dozen drivers had arrived to fill up, and had presented themselves at the till window to pay, the attendant squeezing apologetically in to deal with them. This must be another one.

But now, looking up as the door was vigorously thrust open, she saw none other than Gwendoline Tritton.

Gwendoline Tritton with, in her right hand, a gun.

She rose, a waterspout, to her feet.

'Stay just where you are.'

She obeyed, if to a limited extent, dropping back against the till but now unrelaxed.

The thoughts raced through her head. Here, with Gwendoline Tritton, gun in hand and evidently prepared to use it, here was proof enough of who had conducted the raid on Heronsgate House. Yes, that implacable eighty-year-old had conceived the whole plan, as soon as she had learnt that CA 534, the ideal formidable threat to use, was there to be seized.

And how had she learnt that one vital fact? Easy answer, now I know that she did. The very whereabouts of the CA 534 had been brought to her by this favourite of hers, Maggie Quirke. And how had Maggie learnt it? In bed with poor Christopher Alexander. By teasing and testing that wretched weak-willed boy. And, yes, she had done more than tease the information out of him. She must have got hold of his key to Dr Lennox's smart silver-grey security cabinet. Probably had a duplicate made, and then at the break-in had pretended to jemmy the cabinet open so as to seal off the trail that might lead back to her. All easy enough.

And what had wriggling Christopher done afterwards? He had, even in his just-let-slip confession, drawn attention to the way the top cabinet drawer had been dented as it was opened.

Yes, every step clear now. Up to this moment. This moment with Gwendoline Tritton's gun steadily pointing at me.

'Well, Maggie,' Miss Tritton said, 'I thought it was about time I came to the rescue. I hope I'm not too late.'

From the corner of her eye Harriet caught a flash of white teeth as Maggie Quirke smiled in evidently joyous relief.

'No,' she said. 'You've arrived in the nick of time.' A pause for thought. 'I expect you saw someone nosing into the Mini outside. She's a detective. They've got some crazy idea that I'm concealing something or other that they think's important.'

'Ah, yes. Well, I doubt if she'll get in our way, not with what's in my hand.'

'But how did you manage to know where I was?' Maggie asked then.

'Oh, my dear, that was easy. This stupid woman here had the temerity to answer a call on her mobile thing right inside my house. My house.'

Indignation, however, did nothing to make the pointing pistol quiver by so much as a millimetre, though Harriet was watching it, hawk-intent.

'And you heard on her mobile what was said to her?'

'Better than that, my dear. I heard what she herself said out loud. *Petrol station at this end of University Boulevard* and *I'll be there in ten minutes.*'

Harriet forcibly suppressed the blush of total shame that threatened to come shooting up.

How could I have been such a fool? How could I?

'Not very difficult to realise what had happened to you then,' Miss Tritton went on, drawing herself further up with a little jerk of conceit. 'But it did take me some while to find a way of baffling those idiot police officers all over the house. However...'

Keep on with your self-praise, Harriet thought. Keep on and on with it. Until my moment is there. Or, perhaps, DC Hardy comes back in and sees what's happening quickly enough.

But the gun was still directed at her own chest. A threat not to be taken in any way lightly.

'However,' Miss Tritton went on, the pride in her voice lapping out like rich cream, 'before long I realised that those unpleasant intruders had been working their way up the house, dreadfully methodically, the poor fools, from bottom to top. So my nice old gun would still be there, in my bedroom, in the drawer of my table. Then it was simply a matter of getting it out and tucking it under my jacket. But do you know what I did next?'

'No,' said Maggie, hero-worshipping.

'Hah. I picked up the phone beside the bed and simply called the car-hire company I always use. *Send a car, a Rover if you have one, to The Willows,* I said. *Tell the man to stop outside and give a hoot on his horn. I'll come out straight away.* And my dear, it worked. Like a charm. None of those busily searching policemen noticed me quietly walking by. And here I am.'

Damn. She's told her story. Gwendoline Tritton has put the world in its place. Now, what's she going to do?

The answer came at once. Voice upraised as always.

'Very well, get yourself ready, Maggie, and we'll be off. I don't think Detective Superintendent Martens will attempt to stop us. But, if she does, I won't hesitate to put a bullet in her. When I was a mere child I shot plenty of dying dogs.'

She'll do it, Harriet thought. If she wasn't mad before, she is now. Being in possession of that all-powerful threat in its little tube has pushed this egomaniac one step too far. She'll do anything now to make sure her absurd Waggy gets its way. Her way.

So she had better be stopped.

It's up to me. If I let the threat of that gun prevent me acting, then she'll get away with it. She'll go with bloody Maggie down to London. The pair of them will hide somewhere in all that mess of streets and, when they choose, they'll make their way to some choice fertile spot somewhere and let loose that manipulated stuff. It could be the end of us all.

So, Gwendoline Tritton, you've got to be stopped. Now.

She looked at the gun, pointing at her steadily as ever.

But didn't someone say something to me at some time about Miss Tritton's gun? I've forgotten who, forgotten what. Totally forgotten.

Yes, I'm afraid all right. Fear, stupid fear, has driven everything out of my mind.

That gun. Pistol. It's— It's— If I knew, may be I could... It is a—

Blankness.

Then, in the depths, something at last stirred.

A vague outline of someone, a man, sitting in front of me and saying something about— About a gun. About Miss Tritton's gun.

And... And, yes, he, whoever he was, called her, yes, *That woman.*

It all came back then. DI Weston at the station nearest

The Willows, reciting the full tally of Gwendoline Tritton's misdemeanours. One of which was *being in possession of a firearm without a licence.* A replica gun.

She stepped forward, hand held out.

'I'll have that,' she said. 'You've been warned before about keeping something of that kind.'

Gwendoline Tritton, face in a moment drained of life, simply turned the pistol round and thrust it out, butt-first.

The door of the tiny cramped office opened. DC Emma Hardy looked in.

'I'm sorry, ma'am,' she said, from where she stood not taking in the situation, 'but it's no good. That box, or that tube, is nowhere to be found.'

Harriet's first, totally inconsequential thought was *a fine time for you to come in, DC Hardy*. But at once it dawned on her that it would have made no difference if the poor woman had barged in two or three minutes earlier.

Yes, she might have had a go at Gwendoline. And she would have found, then, that gun was in no way menacing. But the news she brought with her would have been the same. That the CA 534 was *nowhere to be found*.

Perhaps it had never been here to be discovered. Perhaps ferocious Miss Tritton had never handed it to Maggie to sneak out of harm's way. But, wait, she herself might have it with her now. Might have constituted herself personally to be the guardian of the threatening device she had been solely responsible, in her mind, for bringing into action. She could have simply taken it with her, along with her gun, when she went waltzing out of the house. It's in all probability in the hire car out there, its uniformed driver staring respectfully ahead into space.

Must see. But, first, I've got something to do.

'Gwendoline Tritton,' she said. 'I am arresting you on suspicion of being a person who is concerned in the commission of an act of terrorism. You do not have to say anything. But it may harm your defence if you do not mention when questioned something which you later rely on in court. Anything you do say may be given in evidence.'

DC Hardy had got her notebook out, ready.

But Gwendoline Tritton evidently had nothing to say.

Harriet turned her attention to Maggie Quirke, and recited to her the same by rote words. She, too, it seemed, had nothing to say, though something offensive had evidently been on the point of pouring out.

'Right,' she said then to Emma Hardy, 'I think you'd better go out to that hire-car and see what you can find.'

'Ma'am.'

There followed some fifteen minutes with all three women in the office looking at each other in fixed silence. Outside, voices were raised as the grey-capped driver of the Rover was persuaded he had no alternative but to allow his gleamingly polished vehicle to be searched.

Then Emma came back in.

'Nothing, ma'am,' she reported, voice deadened.

Harriet felt it as a blow. But no question of admitting defeat. As a last resort Gwendoline Tritton, old lady though she was, could be subjected to the same intimate search Maggie Quirke had endured. However, there was one more way left yet.

'All right,' she said. 'Then we must trust that DS Jones will make a find at The Willows, though it's hard to see why what you called the *treasure* has been left there. Call him and ask what progress he's made.'

Emma Hardy stepped out of the office to use her mobile.

Clever girl, Harriet recorded. Cleverer by a good deal than the *stupid woman* who repeated Mr Brown's directions to the petrol station here out loud in front of a suspect.

In less than a minute, however, the DC returned, crestfallen.

'Ma'am, they've finished at the house and— And, ma'am, they found the box all right, behind a row of books on the top shelf of some sort of library. But, ma'am, it was empty. No treasure. None at all.'

Harriet caught, like a full-out blow between her eyes, the look of renewed triumph on Miss Tritton's waxen face.

Damn, she thought, should have packed the horrid creature off to a cell soon as I'd made the arrests.

She stepped out to the forecourt. The two PCs were sitting in their car, its doors open to catch the mildly warm Spring breeze, early sandwich lunches on their laps.

'Sorry to spoil your rest,' she called across to them. 'But there are a couple of prisoners inside, and I'd like them taken to the nick at Waterloo Gardens. Say I'll be along shortly to charge them.'

When the two under arrest had been led away – a last contemptuously sneering flash of white-white teeth from Maggie – she went back to disconsolate Emma Hardy.

'I suppose that's it,' she said. 'The finish. I should really have gone along to Waterloo Gardens with those two and seen to charging them. But I somehow still hope there may be somewhere where that test tube could be. You're really happy that there's nowhere in the Rover? Or in the Mini still?'

'Ma'am, I'd up and resign if, at any stage, anybody finds anything in either of those two cars.'

'You're right. I know. I've seen you at work. But, here's a thought. Can that woman Maggie have swallowed the test tube?'

Emma Hardy shook her head.

'Not if it's the dimensions I was given,' she said. 'One of the things we learn in training is what's possible or not possible in that way. And I checked the other possible place of bodily concealment, as you saw.'

Harriet watched then as Emma began packing her search tools into their case, each item carefully put in its place.

Then a notion.

Simple but blindingly obvious.

'No, wait. We haven't finished. Look, aren't there a couple of small things still under the table there, right at the back? In all the excitement I hadn't remembered them.'

Emma stooped down.

'You're right, ma'am,' she said, hollow voiced. 'Two sort of little bags. What looks like a vanity zip-up, plastic, gold, or gold once. Pretty grimy, matter of fact. And then what must be her wash-bag. How could I have forgotten?'

'All right,' she said to Emma, 'go ahead and do your stuff with each of them.'

Emma chose first to deal with the one that looked to Harriet to be the most likely, the scuffed little vanity bag. A fair bet that among all the bits and bobs Maggie would have needed to make herself look pretty, the brand new things and the all but finished ones, there could be, perhaps lightly disguised, that tube of darkly yellow oil.

Probably she's right to pick on that first, she thought. Though, if it was me, I'd have gone for the least likely one, the wash-bag, so as to have all the more luck when it came to the cosmetics-crammed vanity thing, the last possible chance of all. OK, it's superstition. But at a time like this superstition's all you've got.

Yet, leaning intently forward, she watched Emma unzip the vanity bag, tip its contents out on the table and then with active gloved fingers sort rapidly through them. But, trained searcher as she was, before examining the objects she poked and pried at the lining of the bag itself.

'Well, that's out of the way,' she said half a minute later. 'Stuck fast to the outer plastic. So let's have a look at the clutter stuff.'

This operation took longer.

Seeing Emma examining tweezers, nail file, little mirror, pressing and squeezing each brightly coloured tube, opening each pot and expertly wiggling a finger inside, Harriet once again admiring her thoroughness.

But, however miscellaneous the bag's contents, it could hardly take very long to get it to yield up any secret. So it came as no surprise when Emma now turned round from the table.

'Nothing.'

'Try the wash-bag.'

Surely this was the last, last chance.

Emma carefully replaced the contents of the vanity bag before tipping out the items in the sponge-bag. They were not as many of them, a container of contraceptive pills, an ancient wash-cloth, a small 'guest soap' in a little egg-shaped plastic container, an orange plastic razor, a toothbrush, its bristles splayed out, a fat new tube of Aquafresh toothpaste, a round packet of indigestion pills.

Harriet stood there, watching and trying not to watch, as Emma first dealt with the wash-bag itself and then tested each of its contents, however unlikely as a hiding place. Contraceptive pills, even felt at to make certain they were what they seemed to be, the hard-dried wash-cloth, carefully spread out, blade of the orange razor checked as being in place, top taken off the big toothpaste tube, now seen to be unused, its inner metal cap firmly in place, guest soap container opened and the soap sniffed at, however too small it was to conceal the CA 534 tube.

It must have been as long as ten minutes, ten conscientious minutes, before Emma stepped back from the table.

'Blank,' she said, looking straight at the calendar-covered wall in front of her.

'Blank? Blank? But it can't be.'

Yet she knew that *can't be* was mere whistling in the wind. This was the end. The furthest possible distance had been reached. Ultima Thule, the cold region of utter hopelessness.

Then something tickled at the back of her brain. Something, not from the past, but from just a few moments...

White teeth.

Maggie Quirke's white teeth, glinting as she gave me that last contemptuous sneer. But in the wash-bag there had been a big new tube of standard Aquafresh toothpaste, the brand I saw in Christopher Alexander's little bathroom, his tube with the cap left off, the way at home the twins always left uncapped the toothpaste they shared. And beside it, on the spattered shelf above the washbasin, there had been Maggie's own half-used teeth-whitening Arm and Hammer tube.

She pushed past Emma, was about to grab the Aquafresh, then, just in time, recollected what she had been trained years ago to recall about fingerprints. She seized a spare pair of Emma's gloves and picked the Aquafresh up.

Yes, feels solid, just as a new tube should do but I think...

Only one way to find out.

She ripped off, with useless fumbling gloved fingers, the little metal safety tab across the nozzle. Then, holding the tube, nozzle down, over the dirty old table, she squeezed it hard from its base. Squeezed and squeezed. On the grease-stained surface below a long snake of striped toothpaste descended and coiled itself into a slobby multi-coloured mound.

And then stopped.

But the tube was still fat, though not as fat as it had been when she'd picked it up. There was something in it still.

'Emma, you've got a thing that'd get this wide open?'

Without a word in answer the DC flipped open her tools case, selected a small pair of clippers, got to work.

And there a few moments later, on the table, a couple of inches away from the toothpaste mound, was a test tube, filled, it was plain to see despite the dentifrice smears, with a thick yellow oil-like liquid.

Got it. Got it. Got the sole specimen there is of ultra-destructive CA 534.

She felt a wave of gratitude sweep over her.

I did it. I was given a task, almost against my will. And, despite the terrible ever-hovering thought of Graham dead, Malcolm appallingly injured, that task I carried out. To the end. I set aside the Faceless Ones' directive pointing to dear old Ernst Wichmann. I ignored the opposition I got from king-of-the-castle Dr Giles Lennox. And, however unlikely it looked that a piddling outfit like WAGI could be behind that brutal raid at Heronsgate House, I kept them in mind. I saw through the story blarneying O'Dowd cooked up, eventually anyhow, and I leant on poor Winston Earl till he cracked. I took friendly daffodils to unfriendly Aunty Beryl and was rewarded with a statement that blew apart that fifteen-witnesses alibi. Finally I went head-to-head against truly formidable Gwendoline Tritton and at last had the pleasure of seeing her taken into custody. And now I've brought my personally allocated task to its end.

Or, almost.

'Emma,' she said to DC Hardy, standing there looking in some awe at the toothpaste-smeared deadly little test tube, 'all the evidence here is ring-fenced for the prints on it, isn't it?'

'Certainly is.'

'Then label it, like a good girl, and see that you take it, chain-of-evidence unbroken, to safe storage. There's a major trial ahead of us.'

'Will do.'

It had been decided, at very much the last minute, that the funeral should take place in Birchester rather than in London. The Faceless Ones had got hold of, or claimed that they had, information that indicated the group who had 'claimed responsibility' for the bomb behind Notting Hill police station was planning to attack the London crowd expected at St Paul's. So Birchester Cathedral had been hurriedly pressed into service.

Harriet was taken aback by finding the funeral was upon her. John had made himself responsible for all the arrangements that fell to them both, including, she was just aware, informing all the people who had written the letters of condolence he had not so far let her read. Immersed until recently in the therapeutic task Mr Brown had given her, she had hardly given a thought to the actual date.

So it was in a curiously dazed state that she found herself standing outside Birchester Cathedral at some minutes before half-past ten on what had turned out to be a nastily cold morning, swirling with thin but clammy fog. They were, she had just about taken in, waiting for the arrival of the Metropolitan Police contingent who were to take part. Among them – this she did know – would be Malcolm, pronounced fit enough to attend in a wheelchair. Bemused, she looked up now at the elaborately decorated building, a nineteenth century self-tribute to the city, and thought how, on the rare occasions she had been inside it, it had deeply depressed her with its dull red glossy stonework, its narrow shape, its far distant arched roof, and, too, its faint lurking atmosphere of there being, somewhere up there, a God threatening, at any edict disobeyed, eternal hell fire.

And, she added to herself, I'm not going to feel today any of the sentiments proper to the mother of a young man dead before his time. I just don't see why I should. If I am going to feel for Graham, and, by God, I have done, I have done, then I'll do it in my own time and in my own way.

She looked at the queue of people waiting for the closed doors to open, a TV crew off-handedly filming them. Well wrapped up though they were, they all looked pinched with cold. Noses were red. Hands, those that were not gripping open umbrellas, were being surreptitiously rubbed together, as if it was somehow letting down the side to admit to being affected by the damp and dismal air.

'For God's sake,' she muttered to John beside her. 'Can't they open up? It's freezing out here.'

'We've got to wait for the dignitaries from the Met,' he said.

'Fuck the Met.'

'Language, language. Your Mr Brown's not far away.'

'Oh God, sorry.'

She looked behind her. Mr Brown, a pillar figure in brass-buttoned police-blue coat and sternly worn braided cap, was, mercifully, at enough of a distance not to have heard her sacrilegious words. She gave him a tentative smile. And received, despite his rigidly Scottish bearing, a look back that was a good deal warmer.

Well, she said to herself, one good thing about all these past few days, I've come to have a lot of admiration for the ACC. Not many other senior officers would have had the toughness and the compassion, yes, compassion, to have given me work to do. And hard work, too.

Work – she allowed herself a jounce of pride – that I accomplished. To the full.

John leant towards her and murmured.

'And, let me remind you, we, both of us, for this one day or this hour and a half, or whatever it turns out to be, count as dignitaries. Just like the Chief Constable waiting over there.'

'All right. I'll do the proper thing. But I wish the London lot would get a move on.'

'Fog on the motorway, I expect. No. No, here they come.'

A cavalcade of impressive motorcars swept into the cathedral forecourt. The patiently waiting three-abreast queue shifted about in relief.

From the leading car the Commissioner of the Metropolitan Police himself stepped out. A figure Harriet recognised from dozens, if not scores, of newspaper photos and television interviews.

Mr Brown, plainly by arrangement, immediately crossed over to him. They shook hands. Mr Brown said something, inaudible from where they were. But the Commissioner gave him a grave nod and visibly squared his shoulders, yet more heavily braided than the ACC's cap. Then the two of them came heading towards John and herself.

'Harriet,' Mr Brown said, and she was grateful again for the forename, 'Sir Frederick would like a word.'

'Mrs—' Momentary pause, evidently occasioned by his abruptly realising that the Detective Superintendent Martens he thought he was about to speak with was not wearing police uniform but her one and only funeral-going black outfit. 'Er— Mrs Piddock, allow me to offer the deepest sympathies of every one of my officers for the terrible act of which your son was victim.'

She managed a noise that indicated gratitude.

'I would like you to know,' the Commissioner went on, 'that we consider the ceremony here today to be a sign for the whole nation to see that we will not be intimidated by terrorists, of whatever stripe, as long as we have officers as brave and resolute as your son to keep the Queen's Peace.'

Another somewhat confused pause.

'That is, of your two sons, I should say. Police Constable...er...Malcolm Piddock also suffered terrible injuries at the hands of...of those...'

'Thank you, sir,' Harriet said, loudly and clearly.

Thank you for nothing, she allowed herself disrespectfully to think. Damn it, I'm not here because I want to be part of the conveying a message to the great British public.

No, I'm here, in the shape of Hologram Harriet, briefly revived, because a Mrs Piddock ought to be here. A dummy figure.

But, if there's any message Real Harriet wants to *convey*, it's the one I produced during that awful interview on television. Not that we must not be intimidated, but that we should be asking ourselves what in the past we did that has aroused so much anger against us. Yes, even in India, however misguided the people who planted that bomb in Notting Hill.

John, as the Commissioner still escorted by Mr Brown moved towards the now opened doors of the cathedral, leant towards her and, tugging from his pocket one of the terrible little pieces of paper – sometimes even a soft restaurant napkin – on which he scrawled any quotation that particularly struck him, whispered,

'*The honourable justification of violence will always be to me the greatest evil because it makes men blind.* Wonderful Irish novelist, Jennifer Johnston.'

She felt a flush of gratitude. John, clever John, connecting the Commissoner's words with hers in the studio, and finding, scrumpled in his pocket, reassurance.

Then she saw that Malcolm was being lifted in his wheelchair out of the adapted police vehicle that had brought him up to Birchester.

She hurried off towards him, seeing with every step nearer that he did look much fitter than she had feared. There was – she had been able to make out even at a distance – still an ominous patch of white plaster at the side of his head where the piece of flying metal had entered. But otherwise there was only the rug over his legs that perhaps predicted long days of wretchedness ahead.

'Malcolm, are you all right?'

'Oh yes. Yes, I'm fine. Look at me, new uniform brought to St Mary's last night, all bright and shining. And—' He heaved his upper body a little more forward, dropped his voice to a near-whisper, 'guess what I've got, too. A

Policeman's Friend. Really. I didn't know they existed any more, thought they were just a training school joke. But I've got one tucked away here in my trousers. Good idea, really. I'm not in total charge of things down there yet, and if I get wheeled up to where I'm to do my bit and drip pee all over the cathedral, it won't look too good.'

'Malcolm, you're incorrigible.'

But, she thought, no, he isn't. He's wonderful. Tough, not to be beaten. Not by terrorists, not by life.

'Incorrigible? Expect that's what my boss thinks, too. He's over there, heading the lot from the Met, that little shrimp of a fellow.'

Harriet looked. So that's deep voiced, ponderous Superintendent Robertson, I'd never have thought it. And somehow now that fearful telephone message doesn't seem to have been so – what's it? – *portentous*.

John had joined them in time for the naughty tale. He grinned at his son and went to the back of the chair.

'We've got to go in. All set in orders. Commissioner goes first. The Bishop's entering by his own special door. And then we take our places in the front pew, on the left as we approach.'

'Quick march then,' Malcolm said.

They set off.

When they had gone about ten yards Harriet realised something. Something she actually found rather comforting. In motion, Malcolm's chair screeched abominably.

Squeak, squeak, squeak, they went over to the cathedral. There, she found, two burly officers of Greater Birchester Police had been stationed – had they been concealed just inside? – waiting to lift Malcolm in his chair up the steps and into the porch.

Then off they went again up the broad central aisle.

Squeak, squeak.

I will not giggle. I will not giggle.

At last they reached the front pews. John ushered her in

first, manoeuvred Malcolm's chair a bit, slipped in beside her, pulled the chair back till Malcolm was level with them, applied its brake.

Behind, from the organ loft, there came now subdued and all but tuneless music.

John put his lips close to her ear.

'How I hate that moaning noise,' he muttered. 'Always makes me want to jump up and shout *why can't you give us something a bit cheerful?*'

She nodded quick agreement.

Now the main body of the congregation was entering. The sound of discreet words of greeting to and fro came to her ears. Soon to be replaced by the clonking of police boots as the contingent from the Met and a body of officers of the Greater Birchester Police made their way to their allocated pews.

Then the Bishop emerged from his hidey-hole, mitred and crozier-wielding, took his place on his throne.

Now the music-less music dropped in volume and from the open doors at the far end – Harriet in a moment knew what must be coming – there sounded the leaden march of solid feet, the pall-bearers bringing in the coffin. She sat, rigid, where she was, looking straight ahead. At nothing.

But soon, all too soon, she knew that the coffin on the shoulders of its four solid police officers was beside her.

Graham, she thought. Graham is in it. There. But is it Graham? That – it must be – dreadful bundle of broken bits? My Graham. My son. The boy that I bore with Malcolm. The body they mutilated.

Up the two steps and through the gates in the chancel rail the coffin was carried. At last, abruptly transformed into so many ungainly human beings, the bearers contrived to lower their burden on trestles which, hitherto, Harriet had not noticed. They regrouped, solemn once again, dipped their heads as one, moved away.

And there was what the whole elaborate ceremony was about. The body of Police Constable Graham Piddock.

The organ swelled up into a louder version of what had been played earlier. Then was stilled. Coming down to the altar rail was a figure Harriet recognised from various similar occasions in the past, the Greater Birchester Police chaplain.

'Friends,' he intoned reedily.

I just wish he'd call us something a bit less sloppy, she thought with a small spurt of anger.

And at once wondered whether her rage was, in fact, an attempt to keep at bay some deeper true emotion.

'Friends, let us begin by singing what was Graham's favourite hymn, to the words by John Bunyan and music by Sir Edward Elgar, "He who would valiant be".'

The organ boomed off again.

How the hell does he know that was Graham's 'favourite hymn', Harriet asked herself. I don't know that it was. I very much doubt, in fact, if Graham had a favourite hymn.

She leant forward to look at Malcolm. Had he been responsible? But he was sitting blank-faced.

Behind, the congregation, bit by bit, took up the words.

And they came back, in full force, to Harriet. The words that had been embossed on her mind from schooldays, memory-loaded, if not strictly Bunyan's own, at least his thoughts adapted to a more singable shape. *Let him in constancy follow the Master.* Well, I don't think Graham followed in recent years any Master of that sort. But whoever, whatever, he followed, he did so in constancy. And, yes, he was valiant. He was valiant when, with foolish impetuosity, he approached that parcel in Ladbroke Walk. And met that horrible end. At the hands of those deluded idiots who believed by killing other people they could threaten their way into achieving altogether ridiculous ends.

Up at the altar the service droned on.

Harriet still felt totally unaffected. This was something other people had to do, or wanted to do. To register some sort of alliance with dead Graham, Graham the dead victim of just one of those murderous causes.

She hardly listened.

Then suddenly she heard the words, *will be read by the victim's twin brother, Police Constable Malcolm Piddock.* Jesus, Malcolm. Malcolm's going to take part. That's what he must have been talking about outside when he said he would do my bit and then went on to produce his joke about peeing.

But John had leant forward and released the brake on the chair, and now he was slipping out of the pew and beginning to push Malcolm forward. Squeak, squeak, squeak, to be for a few moments the central point of the whole ceremony.

But what's he going to read? I knew nothing of this. I suppose it's part of the arrangements John so decently took off my shoulders. What could he have to read? God knows, he's never been much of a reader himself. Except college stuff. Got him a fair degree. But this... What can it be?

Now, however, squeaky chair safely braked squarely in the chancel with John standing a little back from it, Malcolm raised his head in the hushed silence.

And then came the words. Shakespeare's, often and often said aloud at funerals and never tarnished by that.

> *'Fear no more the heat o' the sun*
> *Nor the furious winter's rages.*
> *Thou thy wordly task hast done,*
> *Home art gone and ta'en thy wages.'*

That was all. All, presumably that John had thought Malcolm, still wracked by weakness and not a little pain, could manage. But they were enough.

Harriet knew that down her cheeks soft tears were now quietly falling.

Yes, now all this, the big echoing cathedral, the people massed into it, the Bishop, the Commissioner, the Chief Constable, the Lord Mayor, Superintendent Robertson, now they all mean something. Now I can do more than rage internally, as I've done ever since I heard that Graham was dead. Now I can mourn. I can start the mourning that, I know, will go on, go quietly on, for the rest of my life.

Some other words of Shakespeare's came into her mind.

After life's fitful fever he sleeps well.
Treason has done its worst, nor steel, nor poison,
Malice domestic, foreign levy, nothing
Can touch him further.

Whose epitaph had that been? King Duncan's? Yes, think it's that. But it applies with time-proofed strength to poor Graham, too. Nothing can touch him now. He's safe from all the threats that fly about our world. He is safe. Poor Graham. Safe Graham.